JUSTICE LEAGUE

Secret Origins

JUSTICE LEAGUE™

Secret Origins

Novelization by

MICHAEL TEITELBAUM

Based on the teleplay *Secret Origins*
by Rich Fogel

BANTAM BOOKS
NEW YORK • TORONTO • LONDON • SYDNEY • AUCKLAND

SECRET ORIGINS

A Bantam Book/August 2002

ISBN: 0-553-48770-1

Visit us on the Web! www.randomhouse.com/kids
Educators and librarians, for a variety of teaching tools, visit us at
www.randomhouse.com/teachers

Visit DC Comics at www.dccomics.com

Published simultaneously in the United States and Canada

Bantam Books is an imprint of Random House Children's Books, a division of
Random House, Inc. BANTAM BOOKS and the rooster colophon are registered
trademarks of Random House, Inc. Bantam Books, 1540 Broadway, New York,
New York 10036.

PRINTED IN THE UNITED STATES OF AMERICA

OPM   10 9 8 7 6 5 4 3 2 1

For my marble-mouthed childhood friend, Lawrence Sokolsky, who came running home from the candy store one Saturday afternoon long ago screaming about a new comic book called Just a Sleek America. *I've been a JLA fan ever since.*

Special thanks to: Rich Fogel, for his terrific story; Bruce Timm and the folks at Warner Bros. Animation for their great show; Marissa Walsh of Random House for her input; and Charlie Kochman of DC Comics for his insight and guidance as "keeper of the characters." —MT

PROLOGUE

Ed Reiss and J. Allen Carter were not the first Earth astronauts to explore Mars, they were simply the latest. Their mission: search for water, the foundation of life throughout the solar system, in the hopes of discovering evidence of intelligent beings somewhere in the planet's history.

Swirling winds skated across the surface of the red planet, whipping ancient dust and soil into tiny crimson tornadoes. Deep in the Mariner Valley—named for the first Earth spacecraft to visit the nearby world—about two hundred yards from their ship, the two explorers bounded easily across the vast expanse, their weight only a third of what it was back home.

Shoving a metal probe into the dirt, Ed Reiss adjusted its settings as best he could while wearing the thick gloves attached to the sleeves of his airtight space suit. Crackling static filled his ears as he studied the readings on the probe.

"Would you look at that, Reiss," a voice said through the radio com-link in his helmet. "A little slice of heaven."

Glancing over his shoulder, Reiss saw his partner taking in the scenery. His arms were open wide, a huge grin visible through his glass face shield.

"Yeah, sure, Carter," Reiss replied. "If your idea of heaven is a barren, lifeless rock." Ed Reiss was a scientist, always had been. If humans had never achieved space travel, he would have been satisfied to do his research on Earth. But since this was the cutting edge of scientific inquiry, Mars was where he had to be, despite his impatience with the long flights and somewhat clumsy working conditions.

"That's my partner," Carter said, laughing, as he turned to the task of setting up his own probe. "You have the soul of a poet." Allen Carter, on the other hand, was an adventurer. If he hadn't qualified for the space program, he'd be in a submarine on the bottom of the ocean, or climbing to the peak of Everest. A solid scientist, Carter's first love was exploration.

"Carter, we didn't come for the view," Reiss pointed out. "Our mission here is purely scientific. Are you getting any readings?"

"No," Carter replied, checking the gauges on his probe. "No detectable levels of H_2O." Looking a short distance away, Carter caught a glimpse of sunlight glinting off a small rock formation. "Hold on!" he called into the com-link. "I may have something."

Bounding toward the formation, enjoying each reduced-gravity leap, Carter squinted at the gleaming object protruding from the oxidized red soil.

"What do you see?" Reiss asked, pulling his probe from the ground.

"Could be an ice crystal," Carter explained, executing a perfect two-footed landing right in front of the outcropping.

Kneeling beside the shining white object embedded in the rocks, Carter pulled his geologist's pick from its loop on his space suit. Slowly, he chipped away the stone from around the object, prying it free with the pick. Carter turned the pointed, melon-sized formation over in his gloved hands.

"No," he reported. "It's not ice. Looks almost organic, like a large bone fragment, maybe a skull."

A rumbling suddenly shook the astronauts where they stood. Beginning as a deep, dull sound, the vibrations grew in intensity, as if something beneath the surface of the planet were trying to get out. Within seconds, the ground under Carter's feet split open, the fissure spreading quickly.

"Carter, look out!" Reiss shouted. His partner dropped the object in his hands and turned to flee.

"What's going on?" Carter yelled back, leaping into the air as the solid footing underneath him cracked like thin ice, spiderwebbing in all directions. Staying just in front of the growing chasm, Carter bounded across the dusty surface, the ground vanishing behind him.

"Hurry!" Reiss cried, watching as the lengthening crack seemed to chase Carter, who struggled to remain on solid ground.

KER-RACK!

Only several yards away from Reiss, Carter's foot stretched out for yet another piece of ground but found only air. With the Martian soil folding away beneath him, Carter plummeted into the everwidening abyss.

"Carter!" Reiss shouted, turning to run from the onrushing destruction, now only a few feet away. "Are you all right! Do you read me? Repeat, do you read me?"

Then, just as quickly and inexplicably as it had begun, the crumbling and cracking stopped. Crimson dust settled silently over the gaping crevasse and its surrounding rubble. Reiss dropped to his knees and peered over the edge of the immense opening into infinite darkness. He shouted once more. *"Carter!"*

Already hundreds of yards beneath the surface, Carter was buffeted by rocks and dust, sunlight fading as he plummeted toward the center of the red planet. Dizziness washed over Carter as he reached for a handhold, an outcropping—anything to stop his seemingly endless descent. He grabbed only dust.

Finally Carter landed, slamming into the rough, rocky bottom of the pit. He was bruised but not seriously injured. Despite the weaker gravity, Carter struggled painfully to his feet, wincing and groaning with the effort. Gazing through his cracked faceplate, he could make out only vague shapes. Reaching up, he flipped on his helmet light. Its powerful beam blazed to life, illuminating the walls of an underground cavern.

Attempting to activate his com-link, Carter spoke in a harsh, raspy voice. "I'm okay, Ed," he announced. "Ed? Come in, Ed!"

Static, then silence.

Realizing he was on his own, Carter turned his head. The light beam from his helmet played across the dark gray chamber, revealing a startling discovery. *This chamber appears to be man-made—or maybe I should say* Martian-*made*, he thought, squinting up at what looked like a door decorated with ornate carvings and strange writing. *In any case, this is no natural cavern.*

The thirty-foot-high door appeared to be the only way in or out of this tomblike enclosure. Carter grasped a round metallic seal in its center and pulled. The smooth disc refused to budge. He tried a different grip, but his fingers fumbled helplessly against the closure, unable to gain any leverage.

Then he remembered his pick.

Reaching around to the loop on his space suit, Carter discovered his tool was no longer dangling in its usual spot. A quick glance around revealed it lying on the floor of the chamber.

Retrieving the pick, Carter worked the edge of its sharp blade behind the door's seal, rocking the curved metal tool until it slipped snugly under the rim of the solid disc. Bracing himself as best as he could in the reduced gravity, Carter yanked on the pick again and again. The seal broke loose, gradually at first, then flying from the door, sending him reeling onto his back.

Thick black smoke poured from the hole where the seal had been. Struggling to his feet, Carter glanced up to see a thin beam of bright light traveling along the carvings on the door. It rose like liquid in a glass tube, pulsating as the smoke around him grew more and more dense.

Backing away, Carter shielded his eyes. The entire door glowed, shaking and throbbing, the intense energy behind it desperate for release.

THOOM!!

Exploding from its housing, the massive door slammed into Carter, driving him back into the far wall of the cavern.

The last things he remembered seeing before losing consciousness were swirling patches of red, black, and gray—and the faint glow of two dull orange eyes.

CHAPTER
1

Two years later...

The sprawling complex of the WayneTech radar substation in Metropolis covered acres of land on the outskirts of town. Dominated by the enormous radar dish in the center of the complex, the facility contained a low building attached to the dish's support platform. Inside were offices and control rooms, mainframe computers, and the most sophisticated radar and satellite-guidance technology available.

Surrounded by a chain-link fence topped with razor-sharp curls of barbed wire, the substation was one of the crown jewels in Bruce Wayne's high-tech industrial empire. But for the past several months,

Bruce had noticed security breaches in the deep-space radar monitoring network.

Wayne Enterprises operated this facility for the federal government. Bruce knew that if he went through official channels, the investigation of these breaches would inevitably get bogged down for months in governmental red tape. And so the owner and CEO of Wayne Enterprises decided to investigate the situation himself.

But not as Bruce Wayne.

A caped figure dashed silently across the roof of the low office building. Glancing furtively left, then right, certain he was unseen, Batman firmly grasped a grill covering an open duct. Yanking it free, he slipped like a shadow into the building.

Swinging acrobatically, then landing noiselessly on a rafter above the complex's main control room, Batman crouched in the darkness, peering down at the four people in the room below.

The WayneTech technicians, clad in their long white lab coats, checked monitors, took readings, and prepared to close shop for another day. A tall, thin tech with floppy blond hair and large round glasses headed up a metal staircase leading to the exit.

"Okay, I'm outta here," the skinny tech said, pausing at the top of the stairs. "Another week in the bag. Remember, Al, Lee, Cynthia, barbecue at my place Saturday night. You're all invited. Venus is rising early, and you know what that means! A wild time is guaranteed for all!"

His fellow technicians turned to the young man, broad smiles plastered on their faces.

"I'm there, Howie," replied Al, a heavyset, bald man, the senior member of the group. "Wouldn't miss it."

"Sounds great," added Cynthia, a large, middle-aged woman, peering over the top of her reading glasses.

"Thanks," chimed in Lee, a thin, dark-haired tech, the youngest of the group. "See you then."

Stopping at the exit, Howie turned back to face his colleagues. "You guys are party animals," he snorted, giggling, then winking and flashing the thumbs-up sign. "Good night!"

As the door closed behind Howie, the three remaining technicians glanced at one another in silent relief, the frozen smiles instantly vanishing from their faces.

Batman gazed down from above, watching intently as Al stood and spoke to the others.

"H'i chalt eed 'vaird go!" he shrieked in a shrill, in-human voice, nodding toward the exit. Then, turning to Lee, he added, *"Gy! Na'chrona tote!"*

The skinny young man nodded, then walked quickly to a bank of large mainframe consoles lining the back wall.

Batman's mind raced. He'd been all over the world, heard hundreds of languages, but this speech was completely foreign to him. Shifting his position to get a better view, Batman wondered why this crew would suddenly stop speaking English when Howie left the room.

Grasping an enormous console towering ten feet in the air, Lee easily lifted the weighty piece of equipment, moving it aside as if it were an empty cardboard box.

Cynthia strode to the space vacated by the console, reached up with her right hand, and punched a hole in the thick stone wall. Shoving her arm into the hole, she lifted out an odd-looking piece of technology about the size of a large roasting pan but irregularly shaped, covered with swirling patches of red, black, and gray circuitry.

"Reeg ear a' chai," she announced, carefully cradling the device in her arms.

Stepping toward the wall, Lee placed the console back in the spot from which he had taken it. He then followed the others through a side door leading out onto the support platform that held the massive radar dish in place.

Scowling, Batman climbed back up through the rafters, slipping out onto the roof.

The support platform consisted of four long, narrow metal walkways radiating out from the central radar dish, then curving down to the ground like the long steel legs of a giant spider. Reaching the radar dish, the technicians placed the device they had carried onto the dish's transmitter. Appearing to move under its own power, the apparatus split into four equal sections, then slithered, as if alive, into four openings in the transmitter, vanishing into the depths of the complex radar tracking system.

Satisfied, the three colleagues turned to leave.

"I doubt that modification's legal," a deep, firm voice said from behind them.

Swinging around in shock, they spotted Batman poised at the end of the dish's platform.

Moving with lightning speed, before the three techs could react, Batman sent a rope tether speeding through the air. Finding its target, the tether bound

Al and Lee together as two heavy steel balls attached to each end of the rope spun around and around, faster and faster, tightly securing the two men.

"Shriiiiiiii!" they both screeched, releasing high-pitched, unearthly cries.

"Should've stuck to your desk jobs," Batman announced, dashing toward Cynthia, who stood her ground, her face angry and defiant.

Reaching out to grab Cynthia, Batman recoiled as the female tech swiped at him with surprising speed and power. Dodging the swift backhanded blow, Batman countered with a powerful punch of his own.

Exhibiting extraordinary strength, Cynthia caught Batman's hand midblow, then lifted him by the wrist, tossing him aside like a rag doll.

Reacting instinctively, Batman shifted his weight in midair, whipped his feet around, and landed back on the narrow steel platform in time to see Al and Lee undergo a strange transformation.

Firmly bound by the tether, the two techs reshaped their bodies, sending weight from their midsections up toward their heads, causing the ropes that had held them to slip to the ground. Stepping free of the restraints, Al and Lee redistributed their weight again, resuming their normal human forms.

"Ga' raim!" Al shrieked, pointing at Batman.

Enraged, Cynthia charged at the Dark Knight, who leapt backward in the air while pulling a Batarang from his Utility Belt.

Still in the air, Batman tossed the bat-shaped weapon down toward Cynthia. His eyes widened in disbelief as the spinning Batarang struck her full force in the forehead, then bounced away harmlessly.

Landing on the edge of the platform, Batman had hardly regained his balance when Lee charged furiously toward him like an enraged rhino. Crashing into the Dark Knight, Lee sent him flying off the thin platform, tumbling toward the ground some two hundred yards below.

Focusing with meditative calmness, Batman fired a grappling line from his Utility Belt, the weighted hook at the end catching on the lip of the platform. Pulling himself back up, he swung onto the deck, poised for the next onslaught.

A pair of bright red boots dropped suddenly into view, halting in midair in front of Batman's face.

"Need a hand?" asked a familiar voice.

"Thanks," Batman replied, his eyes locked on his three motionless adversaries. "But I can handle this."

Superman glided gently to the platform, landing

next to his longtime friend and ally. The two great heroes had fought many battles together, engaging enemies of all kinds, taking on creatures from many worlds. On patrol around Metropolis, Superman had spotted this scuffle and figured he'd drop by to lend a hand.

"Ga' raiii!" shouted Al, catching sight of the Man of Steel. Then the three techs turned and ran, with Batman racing after them.

"They don't look so tough," said the Man of Steel, smiling. "Two overweight, middle-aged scientists and a skinny kid shouldn't pose much of a problem for the Dark Knight of Gotham."

Gliding into the air, preparing to leave, Superman was suddenly struck by a searing pain in his head. Clutching his temples with both hands, he jerked, struggling to remain airborne. A flood of vague, distorted images filled his mind, a mental assault from which he had no defense.

"Yaaaa!" Superman cried out, unable to stop the pictures bombarding his brain. At first unclear, several scenes came into momentarily sharp focus, burning deep into his consciousness:

The expansive crimson plains of Mars.

A thriving city on the red planet, filled with buildings, flying vehicles, and a bustling population of millions.

That same Martian city, under attack, blaster fire destroying tall buildings.

A bizarre creature, bloblike, with swirling colors dancing inside an ever-changing skin, its whipping tentacles crackling with energy.

A flaming asteroid streaking across the night sky over a desert on Earth.

A pair of glowing orange eyes beaming from a shadowy face.

All of these images forced their way into his mind within the span of seconds.

Overcome and unable to find his equilibrium, Superman crashed onto the platform in a twisted, writhing heap.

Hearing his friend's scream, then feeling the steel platform shake from the impact of Superman's body, Batman stopped short, giving up his chase. "Superman!" he cried, turning and racing back to his fallen comrade.

Realizing that Batman had stopped coming after them and that Superman no longer posed a threat, Al turned to face the others. *"Gow Hot!"* he yelled, while pulling a small remote-control device from the pocket of his lab coat, aiming it at the radar dish, and pressing a button.

KA-THOOOM!!

Deep inside the dish's transmitter, the strange mechanism they had planted earlier exploded, tearing a huge chunk from the massive dish, destabilizing the four support platforms in the process.

As flames poured from the devastated radar dish, Batman felt the platform buckle. In seconds, the Dark Knight reached the unconscious form of Superman. Ducking to avoid searing chunks of flaming debris, Batman quickly draped Superman's arm over his shoulder and lifted the Man of Steel to his feet. Glancing back, he saw the three technicians, or whatever they really were, leap from the collapsing platform without regard for what would happen when they hit the ground hundreds of feet below.

SWOOOSH!

A huge, sizzling piece of metal buzzed past just above Batman's head, trailing smoke behind it. Feeling the platform about to topple, Batman leapt off. Keeping a firm grip on Superman with one hand, he fired a grappling line back to the falling structure, gaining just enough tension to soften the blow as the two heroes hit the ground.

KA-RAKK!!

The entire support platform crumbled as Batman and Superman, separated now, tumbled down a hill, away from the smoldering complex. Over and over they rolled in a dizzying free fall, unable to stop their momentum.

Slamming into a grove of trees, Batman groaned as he finally stopped tumbling. Superman crashed into a tree stump a few feet away. Forcing himself up on one elbow, Batman watched incredulously as the three techs stood up in a charred, smoke-filled hole in the ground near the base of the now-fallen radar platform. Their bodies were horribly mangled.

One by one, the beings who called themselves Al, Lee, and Cynthia snapped their twisted, misshapen heads, arms, and legs back into normal human positions, brushing off their fall as if it had never happened. As the three strolled casually into the nearby woods, Al turned back toward Batman. He winked, flashed the thumbs-up sign, then disappeared with the others into the forest.

Batman crawled painfully over to where Superman lay sprawled on the ground. As he reached his friend, he saw Superman's eyes flutter open. The Man of Steel sat up, grabbing his throbbing head.

"What happened?" he groaned, rubbing his temples.

"You tell me," Batman replied, slowly getting to his feet. He knew that Superman was not invulnerable to all the forces of the universe, but it always took him by surprise to see the great hero toppled and suffering with pain.

"I don't know," Superman said, feeling his strength return a bit. "I saw images. Another planet, some kind of attack. So intense. And then, then . . . I don't know. That's all I remember. It's as if I was attacked by the images, as if someone forced them into my mind."

Batman helped Superman to his feet, then pointed to the smoking, decimated radar dish. "Obviously, they didn't want to leave evidence behind, whoever they were."

"What's all this about?" Superman asked, surveying the damage.

"Over the past few months, I've detected several security breaches in our global deep-space monitoring network," Batman explained. "Many of them could be traced to this facility. And now with the destruction of the radar dish, it's pretty clear that someone doesn't want us looking out into the cosmos."

"Any idea who?" Superman asked.

"No," Batman replied, kneeling down to the ground, picking up a tiny piece of red, gray, and black circuitry with a pair of tweezers. He dropped the sample into a small plastic pouch, which he then tucked into his Utility Belt. "There's more to this than meets the eye."

"I'd like to stay and help you look into it, but I'm expected back in Metropolis," Superman explained.

"Getting another key to the city?" Batman asked, straight-faced, never one to pass up an opportunity to poke a little fun at his superpowered friend.

Ignoring the remark, Superman reached into a secret pocket in his cape and pulled out a beeping watch.

"Here," he said, handing the watch to Batman. "It's a signal watch. Call me if you need any more help." Without another word, Superman shot into the sky, fading swiftly from view.

"Right," Batman muttered disdainfully, glancing down at the watch and scowling. Unlike Superman, Batman had no superpowers. The watch was an unwelcome reminder of his mortality, a symbol representing the fact that there might come a time when he encountered a situation that was beyond even his great talent. He glanced over at the twisted, smoldering ruins of the radar dish, then peered into the woods at the spot into which his surprisingly powerful adversaries had fled.

Sighing, he slipped the signal watch into his Utility Belt.

The World Assembly Building in downtown Metropolis rose proudly among the many gleaming towers of the great city's skyline. Conceived as a forum where the nations of the world could meet to settle conflicts through discussion and negotiation, the international organization had its fair share of problems.

Getting representatives from more than one hundred countries to sit down together in the same room was difficult enough. Getting them to agree on solutions to the key problems of the day seemed at times an almost impossible feat. Yet all the delegates from the various nations did agree on one thing—the world had a better chance of surviving with the World Assembly in place than without it.

A meeting of the Assembly's delegates was in session inside the tall steel-and-glass structure. Just outside the building, in Freedom Plaza—long a place of public gatherings, where dissenting voices came to be heard—a group of protesters congregated to express their disagreement with the policies of the organization. Carrying homemade signs and banners reading BAN THE BOMB!, WE WANT A SAFE WORLD!, and DISARM NOW!, the crowd of mostly young people chanted and shouted, led by a bearded man in a stocking cap and a T-shirt that read PEACE NOW!

"They've stockpiled enough nuclear missiles to destroy our entire planet!" the leader shouted into a megaphone, his voice booming to the back of the crowd. "And yet they continue to build more. We demand they stop this madness!"

Picking up his cue, the throng rhythmically chanted, "Stop the madness! Stop the madness!" again and again.

In the large assembly hall on the thirty-fifth floor of the building, other voices were raised as well. The round hall was filled with several levels of curved desks arranged in concentric circles around a central platform. Filled nearly to capacity, the grand hall housed representatives from most of the world's major powers—ambassadors, senators, and military leaders discussing the very same issues being voiced by the protesters outside.

Rising to his feet, the Japanese ambassador waited a moment for the room to quiet, then spoke forcefully. "Weapons of mass destruction," he began, the passion unmistakable in his voice, "my people believe a lasting peace can only be achieved by eliminating them."

"Nonsense!" boomed a voice from across the room. A tense murmur spread through the chamber. All eyes turned to a large man wearing the uniform of the U.S. Army. General's stars decorated his chest. He leapt to his feet almost before the ambassador's words had finished echoing around the hall. "Those weapons are our only defense against aggression!" the general announced, pointing an accusing finger at the Japanese ambassador and scowling, his leathery skin creasing as he stared intently at his adversary.

Whirling to face the general, the Japanese ambassador returned his stare. "Is this your country's official position?" he asked angrily. The ambassador had never been happy about the fact that the World Assembly was on U.S. soil, and now he found this man of war speaking for the host nation just about intolerable.

"No!" came the reply from a man striding onto the hall's main platform. The tall, handsome man in his midforties, dressed in a conservative suit and tie, stepped up to the podium. "General Welles does not speak for our government."

As everyone in the room turned to focus on the man on the podium, General Welles remained standing. "But Senator Carter," he protested. "Only a fool would—"

The senator raised his hand quickly, silencing the general's objection. J. Allen Carter had enjoyed a meteoric rise from astronaut and hero to U.S. senator, gaining a great amount of power in just two short years. He was not about to let a hotheaded general ruin his carefully crafted plans. "General," Carter began, "when I was an astronaut on Mars two years ago, I survived an experience that profoundly changed my life."

General Welles reluctantly took his seat as the hall fell silent.

"Looking back at Earth from the surface of another planet, I saw for the first time how small and fragile our world really is," Carter continued, opening his arms toward the assembled delegates. "I realized that its fate is in our hands. Ladies and gentlemen, that is a responsibility we must not take lightly."

Sensing the hopeful tone in Carter's voice, the members of the assembly leaned forward, hanging on his every word.

"Therefore," he went on, speaking slowly for dramatic effect, "I propose a bold new solution for peace. My plan would use a force more powerful than any before." Pausing, he nodded toward the back of the assembly hall.

"A force dedicated to the safety of all humankind," he said as the doors to the hall swung open. "A force known to all as Superman!"

The assembly let out a collective gasp. When Senator Carter began speaking of a new peace solution, no one expected anything like this. The Man of Steel flew slowly into the hall, carrying a large globe in one hand and waving to the stunned delegates with the other.

Looking up in awe, the diplomats followed Superman's flight. As he slowly drifted to the central platform, all thoughts of their differences vanished for the moment. They were simply delighted to be in the presence of Earth's greatest hero.

All except for General Welles. *Carter sure has a flair for the dramatic*, the general thought, rising slowly to his feet. *I have to give him that. But showmanship and symbolism are not the answers.* "With all due respect, Senator," Welles began, speaking loudly, his sharp voice slicing through the elated mood of the crowd, "we can't entrust the security of the entire world to one man."

Superman landed gently on the platform, placed the globe beside him, and stepped up to the microphone on the podium. "I understand your feelings, General," he said, looking directly at Welles. "I was reluctant to get involved when Senator Carter first approached me. But after meeting with him and his advisors, I became convinced that I could make a difference."

Raising his right hand, palm facing outward, Superman appeared to be taking an oath. "I've fought hard over the years to earn your trust," he continued. "And I solemnly swear to all of you that I will continue to uphold the ideals of Truth and Justice, not just for America, but for all the world."

Overwhelmed by his words, the delegates leapt to their feet as one, applauding loudly, their cheers filling the hall in a resounding endorsement. Cries in many languages rang out, and shouts of "Hooray!", "Thank you, Superman!", and "This is the answer to our prayers!" blended with the thunderous ovation.

General Welles stared at Senator Carter, the outrage in his face met by a calm smile from the senator.

Seemingly borne by the energy in the hall, Superman and Senator Carter strode from the platform, out the main doors, and into the lobby of the building, followed closely by the still-cheering delegates. Gathered around the World Assembly emblem—a globe surrounded by olive branches symbolizing peace—emblazoned on the lobby's marble floor, the ecstatic diplomats huddled around Superman, each eager to shake his hand and offer thanks.

Senator Carter grasped Superman's hand firmly as flashbulbs popped in a random light show, a classic photo op for the powerful politician, an image he knew would grace the front pages of newspapers around the world.

The Japanese diplomat, so hopeful during his emphatic call for the elimination of weapons worldwide, then so bitter upon hearing the unofficial response from General Welles, stepped up to Superman, bowing in gratitude. "Thank you, Superman," he offered. "You have brought hope to all of us."

The Man of Steel respectfully returned the bow, graciously accepting the thanks.

CHAPTER
2

Clark Kent tossed his shirt and pants onto an over-stuffed chair in the corner of his bedroom, then flopped onto his bed, grabbing the remote and flipping on the TV. Sighing deeply, he propped a pillow behind his head, marveling at the fact that even a man of steel can feel beat after a full day of living a double life as a reporter and as Superman.

Six months had passed since his historic address before the World Assembly. During that time, he'd been even busier than usual. In addition to his work at the *Daily Planet* and WGBS-TV as well as his usual crime-fighting duties, Superman had been traveling the world, disarming each nation's stockpile of nuclear weapons.

Clark knew that tonight's newscast would feature a six-month progress report on his disarmament efforts, and he was curious to see how his labors would be portrayed by the media.

Smirking slightly as the logo for *The Carr Report* flashed across his screen, Clark settled back and watched the handsome, sharp-featured news anchor with the mop of dark brown hair face the camera and confidently launch into his evening's broadcast.

"Good evening," the newscaster began. "This is Snapper Carr reporting. It has now been six months since Senator Carter's dramatic disarmament plan was ratified. Superman has been working tirelessly, disarming hundreds of deadly warheads around the world."

Clark yawned, then smiled at the mention of his "tireless" efforts. He watched as footage of Superman ripping the cover off a warhead, fusing its circuits with his heat vision, then tossing the useless weapon aside unfurled on the screen. The camera panned over to a large pile of disarmed missiles, the result of Superman's hard work. The same scene was repeated at various locations around the world.

"Meanwhile," Snapper Carr continued, "public support for the plan has swelled."

The image on the TV screen switched to a shot of Carr himself on the street, interviewing the leader of the protest movement, the same man who had been shouting in Freedom Plaza on the day of the summit.

"Superman rocks!" the young man exclaimed, flashing the two-fingered peace sign at the camera.

"Yet, there are some who remain skeptical," Carr pointed out.

A red blur streaked across Clark's screen, stopped suddenly, then materialized into the super hero known as the Flash, standing on a Metropolis sidewalk being interviewed by Snapper Carr.

"Hey, the big guy's heart's in the right place," the Flash said into Carr's microphone. "But gimme a break. *I'm* the fastest man alive . . ." The Flash dashed off the left side of the screen, vanishing in a heartbeat, then reappearing seconds later, zipping in from the right side, stopping next to Carr. ". . . and even I can't be in five places at once. Although the weather in Paris is very nice this evening, unlike Hong Kong, where it's pretty cold tonight. Hey, gotta run!"

FOOOSH!

The Flash darted away, appearing as a momentary

red smudge on the screen. Clark laughed softly and shook his head as the news report returned to Snapper Carr live in the studio.

"Still, with more missiles being dismantled every day," Carr said, launching into his wrap-up, "most of us will sleep better tonight knowing that Superman is watching over us."

FOOP. Clark tapped the Off button on his TV's remote, the screen going black as he settled back in bed, a satisfied smile spreading across his face. *A pretty fair representation of my work,* Clark thought, reaching for the lamp on his night table.

Switching off the light, Clark breathed deeply and closed his eyes.

Suddenly a searing pain exploded in his head for the second time. As during the incident on the radar dish, the flood of images pouring through his mind felt like an attack against his very existence.

Again, scene after scene forced its way into his brain like a series of rapidly flashing snapshots:

The Earth in space, rising over the scarlet surface of Mars, as if he were standing on the red planet.

A whiplike tentacle, sparking with electric energy.

The door to an underground chamber, sealed with

a large round metallic disc covered in complex carved patterns.

A fiery explosion in a barren stretch of desert.

A fenced-off military compound built into the side of a mountain, with overturned trucks and tanks scattered around the site.

And, once again, the flood of images ended with a pair of glowing orange eyes beaming from a hidden face, burning a hole in his brain.

Bolting upright in bed, drenched in cold sweat, Clark clutched his head in his hands, breathing heavily, desperately searching his mind for the meaning of this latest mental assault.

Moving like a shadow through the murky Metropolis night, Batman's plane, the Batwing, slowed, then silently came to rest on the roof of a deserted building. Once a thriving facility in the S.T.A.R. Labs electronics empire, this rundown factory now sat empty—or so it appeared.

In the months following the attack on the WayneTech radar substation, Batman had scoured the wreckage for clues. He followed many leads, spending endless hours in the Batcave, researching, testing hypotheses, analyzing data, slowly piecing together the puzzle, using his vast array of skills as the World's Greatest Detective.

His hard work had finally paid off, leading him to this desolate structure in a seedy industrial neighborhood on Metropolis's west side. Emerging from the sleek black Batwing, Batman pried open a filthy window, slipped into the building, and swung down on a bat-line, dropping silently to the factory's floor.

Examining a workstation, he spotted several pieces of half-assembled equipment resembling the fragments of circuits he had found among the wreckage of the radar platform, each containing the now-familiar red, gray, and black swirling patterns.

Muffled voices from an office across the factory floor sent Batman shuffling to the shadows, his back pressed against a wall as the office door swung open, flooding the room with light.

"Ra' aza too dacha," announced the man who had called himself Al during his employment with WayneTech. He stepped from the office, followed closely by Lee, then Cynthia, who flipped off the light, closing the door behind her. The three walked quickly from the building.

When quiet returned to the factory, Batman hurried

across the dusty cement floor. Reaching the office, he slipped inside, pulling a small flashlight from his Utility Belt. Its narrow beam revealed a horrific sight.

Squinting in disbelief, Batman moved closer to three large podlike sacs hanging from the ceiling. Through the sacs' translucent shell he saw what appeared to be human bodies, floating in a viscous liquid.

Recovering from the initial shock, Batman whipped out a razor-sharp Batarang and sliced open the sac closest to him. Falling slowly through the thick, mucus-like substance in which it had been floating, the body inside slipped out, crashing to the floor with a dull thud, landing facedown.

Flipping the body over, Batman opened his eyes wide again when he realized that he was staring at Al, whom he had just seen leave the building. Apparently this was the *real* Al.

Kneeling beside him, feeling for a pulse, Batman discovered that the man was not dead, just unconscious, lost in a very deep trance. Looking back up at the two other sacs, no doubt containing the bodies of the other real technicians, the Dark Knight heard a low, menacing growl.

Whirling and leaping to his feet in one swift motion, Batman saw an enormous black rottweiler charging toward him. Moving faster than Batman had realized, the beast was on him in a flash, pinning his back to the floor. The dog lunged desperately toward him, its jaws snapping viciously just inches from his face.

Using all his strength, his hands pressed against the dog's chest, Batman crawled backward, turning his head left, then right, to avoid the deadly razor-sharp fangs. Pulling his knees up to his chest in preparation, then slipping his feet under the rott-weiler, Batman unleashed a powerful thrust with his legs, sending the beast sailing across the room and crashing into a large metal desk.

Recovering with remarkable speed, the dog charged again at full tilt. His back pressed against a cinder-block wall, Batman timed his jump perfectly, waiting until the last second, then leapt straight up and perched on an overhead pipe as the racing ca-nine slammed into the wall.

Again unfazed, the rottweiler looked up and snarled at Batman, then scrambled up the wall toward him. As the beast climbed, it changed, growing larger at first, then shifting its shape, transforming from the familiar figure of the muscular dog into something strange and monstrous—a creature not of this world.

Moving up the wall swiftly, its four limbs somehow finding traction on the painted surface, the alien attacker reached Batman in seconds, knocking him from the pipe. Tumbling toward the ground below, the Dark Knight bounced off a high wall, then crashed into a rusty metal drum, landing on the solid cement floor.

The remarkably agile creature dropped to the floor beside him. Its huge head, long teeth, big chest, and swirls of red, gray, and black filled Batman's blurred field of vision.

Swatting at Batman with a powerful paw, the beast sent him hurling through an interior window, shards of shattered glass exploding everywhere. Sliding across the floor in the next room, Batman crashed into a tall bookcase and toppled the massive wooden structure over onto him, knocking the breath from his battered body.

Fumbling painfully with his Utility Belt, the fingers of his one free hand grasped the signal watch Superman had given him months earlier. Struggling to stay conscious, Batman pressed a tiny button on its side just before blacking out.

Unable to sleep following the second psychic attack, Clark Kent leaned over his bathroom sink, cold water gushing from the faucet. Staring into the mirror at his weary eyes, he cupped his hands, tilted his head, and splashed water on his face again and again.

As Superman, he had faced foes of all kinds, enemies with great power and weapons of inconceivable force. But these latest assaults were different. Somehow, someone had found a way to get inside his head, to barrage his mind with painful blows and disturbing images—and at the moment, there seemed to be nothing he could do about it.

Grabbing a towel and dabbing his face, Clark was suddenly alarmed by the faint beeping picked up by his superhearing.

The signal watch, he realized instantly. *I didn't think Bruce would ever use it. Something must* really *be wrong.*

Putting aside his own problem for the moment, Clark donned his red and blue suit and took to the sky above Metropolis. He was almost glad for the break from his own troubles, though he was quite worried about his old friend.

With his superhearing focused on the steady signal of the watch, Superman followed the frequency, weaving between skyscrapers, heading west as the sound grew louder.

Arriving at the S.T.A.R. Labs factory, the Man of Steel flew through the open window Batman had used earlier and landed on the building's open main floor. A quick scan of the area with his X-ray vision revealed Batman pinned beneath the heavy book-case, left for dead by his alien assailant.

"Oh, no," Superman muttered, dashing to the bookcase, tossing it aside with ease, then kneeling down next to his fallen comrade.

Batman groaned weakly as Superman slowly lifted his head. Blood was smeared across his face and cowl.

"Batman!" the Man of Steel cried, glad that at least his friend was still alive. "I'm going to get you to a doctor right away."

Scooping Batman gently into his arms, Superman turned to leave—just as a giant flaming asteroid ap-peared, impossibly, outside the window, lighting up the night sky.

CHAPTER 3

KA-THOOM!!

The massive asteroid slammed into the center of Metropolis, tearing a trench through dozens of city blocks, spewing flaming destruction in its wake before finally coming to rest.

Speeding from the factory, heading toward the rising flames in the distance, Superman wondered what new horror had struck his beloved city. He was also still extremely concerned about getting Batman some help.

The wail of sirens split the night as emergency vehicles raced to the scene of horrendous devastation. Cars screeched to a halt just inches from the smoldering surface of the enormous asteroid, which protruded from the asphalt, rising ten stories into the sky. Terrified drivers and passengers fled, confused by the surreal sight of the massive rock in the middle of their city.

Arriving at the impact site, Superman was momentarily overwhelmed by the suddenness and scope of the destruction. Spying an ambulance parked by a curb, Superman dropped from the sky. An EMS worker who was pulling a stretcher from the back of the ambulance was startled by the Man of Steel's sudden arrival. He gingerly placed Batman on the stretcher.

"He needs help, medic," Superman said, gently laying Batman's head on a pillow.

"What happened?" the paramedic asked, staring in shock at the two costumed heroes.

"I'm not sure," Superman replied, vanishing in a red and blue blur before the EMS worker could say another word.

Pulling out her stethoscope, the young paramedic listened to Batman's lungs and heart. Satisfied that his breathing and heartbeat were normal, she removed the instrument from her ears, allowing it to drop to her shoulders. Tempted by curiosity and an apparent once-in-a-lifetime opportunity, she slowly reached for Batman's mask.

His gloved hand shot up, clamping on the medic's wrist with a viselike grip. She gasped, terrified by the firm grasp and iron will of the bloodstained hero. "Don't even think about it," he warned.

The medic nodded rapidly, and Batman released his grip. Slowly, she proceeded with her first-aid treatment, working nervously as Batman's piercing gaze followed her every move.

WHUP-WHUP-WHUP-WHUP!!!
WHEE-WHEE-WHEE-WHEE!!!

Police helicopters rushed past overhead, and fire trucks screamed to the crash site—a huge gash in the ground that stretched back for half a mile from the immense asteroid. Leaping from their trucks, firefighters connected their hoses and set about dousing the flames in the many buildings ignited by the arrival of the unwelcome visitor from space. Then they turned their attention to the fires that still engulfed the asteroid itself.

Among the multitude of official vehicles arriving on the scene, a TV remote truck screeched to a halt.

Snapper Carr rushed from the truck, his cameraman two steps behind him. Reaching a line of barricades, Carr joined the other reporters on the scene and leaned forward, his microphone extended.

"Any statements?" shouted one newspaper reporter.

"Where did it come from?" Snapper Carr asked. "Will the governor call for a state of emergency?"

Ignoring the rapid-fire questions, the police struggled to hold back the eager swarm of journalists.

The firefighters soon had the asteroid's blaze under control. Although flames were no longer visible, rippling waves of heat and acrid, foul-smelling smoke still poured from its craggy surface.

Two police officers in full riot gear peered into the trench, then craned their necks to look up at the enormous boulder.

"Look at the size of that thing," one cop commented, leaning closer for a better look.

"Stay back," his partner warned. "It's still incredibly hot."

As the two officers looked on, a burst of black smoke gushed from a crack suddenly forming in the side of the asteroid.

"What's going on?" the first cop wondered, staring at the widening crevice on the rock's surface.

A huge mechanical limb, at least as tall as the asteroid itself, burst forth from the crack, like a giant creature hatching from an enormous egg. It was thick and white, covered with swirling patches of gray, red, and black circuitry, and extended from the asteroid high over the officers' heads.

As the cops gaped in astonishment, the massive metal leg bent downward, its wide foot threatening to crush them where they stood.

Both men screamed, frozen with fear. Suddenly, a red and blue streak swooped down from the sky, gathered the cops up, and carried them to safety. The massive alien leg slammed into the ground, shaking the earth, toppling barricades, officers, and reporters.

"Hang on!" Superman shouted, grasping the two cops firmly, then touching down a short distance away.

Superman looked back at the asteroid in time to see another crack form in its surface and a second identical leg protrude through the opening, heading toward Snapper Carr's remote TV truck.

Standing his ground, Carr watched the mechanical leg approach, yelling back to his cameraman, "Did you get that shot? I want this footage!" Scrambling for cover at the last second, Carr looked back to see the leg squash his empty truck as if it were made of paper. His cameraman captured the devastation for the whole world to see.

As millions watched on TV, a third leg bashed through the rocky crust of the asteroid, followed by a giant, kidney-shaped pod that rested like a strange misshapen head atop the three legs. Now completely free from the asteroid, the huge robotic creature extended to its full height, towering twenty stories above the pavement.

"Incredible!" Snapper Carr reported as the terrible images before him were beamed around the globe. "It appears to be some kind of machine."

A section of the walking pod opened, a dark red circle expanding in its center.

"Something seems to be opening on the machine, and—"

ZZZZ-ZAKK!! THOOM!!

Without warning, a searing plasma blast shot from the eyelike opening, vaporizing two nearby police cars and tossing a third into the air. The car plummeted back to earth, then exploded in a blazing orange fireball.

The police opened fire on the pod with every available weapon, but their bullets bounced harmlessly off the menacing alien invader.

"It appears that the police can't stop this monster," Carr told his viewers. "And this reporter wonders if anything can!"

As if on cue, Superman streaked toward the pod, fists clenched, eyes focused intently on its deadly aperture. The pod fired another blast, striking Superman squarely in the chest, driving him backward through the sky.

Skidding across a rooftop, the Man of Steel tumbled helplessly, crashing into the sidewalk, opening a small crater from the impact of his landing. A crowd quickly gathered around the fallen hero, stunned that Earth's greatest champion appeared to be powerless against this seemingly unstoppable malevolent force.

As the police continued their ineffective barrage, the walker pod crushed squad cars and emergency vehicles, firing plasma blasts at buildings and people. Ignoring the devastation raining down all around him, Snapper Carr shouted at his cameraman, who gawked at the approaching monster, slack-jawed and stunned.

"Come on, stay focused!" Carr yelled. "Are you getting this thing?"

Shaken back to the task at hand, the cameraman lifted his camera to his eye, and once again images of the destruction flashed around the world.

Back at the ambulance, the paramedic worked quickly, cleaning Batman's wounds.

"From the looks of those scars, you've already been stitched back together once or twice," she commented, disinfecting a cut on Batman's arm.

THOOM!

A scorching plasma blast slammed into a building just above them, sending smoking chunks of stone, steel, and glass cascading onto the street surrounding the stretcher.

As the medic looked up in alarm at the burning building, Batman pressed a signaling device on his Utility Belt, commanding the Batwing to autopilot its way to a position directly overhead. When the bat-shaped jet arrived, the Dark Knight raised his arm and fired a grappling Batarang that attached to the underside of the aircraft; then he shot straight up off the gurney, pulled by the thin rope toward the waiting plane.

The medic spoke before glancing back down. "We'd better get out of here before—"

Turning back to her patient to finish her thought, she saw only an empty stretcher.

"Batman?" she asked, looking around, her voice filled with wonder. Glancing back up, she spotted her patient vanishing into the open bay doors in the bottom of the Batwing.

The doors slid shut, and Batman zoomed into the fray.

As police units scattered, scrambling to survive the relentless onslaught, the rampaging pod fired random plasma blasts, destroying buildings in sweeping attacks. Batman lined up his targeting computer as the Batwing swooped toward the pod; then he fired two stinger missiles.

The powerful warheads streaked toward the center of the pod.

KA-THOOM!

Detonating against the walker simultaneously, the missiles erupted in flaming blasts, engulfing the alien battle machine in fire. But when the smoke cleared, the powerful missiles had not even dented the pod's thick hull.

And now the towering walker was aware of a new adversary.

Following the Batwing as it circled for another pass, the pod fired plasma blasts at the speeding craft. Banking sharply, wiggling the jet's wings, Batman narrowly avoided the return fire. *How do we stop this thing?* he wondered as he manipulated the plane.

Three blocks away, Superman slowly climbed from the hole he had created with his landing. Straining with the effort, the Man of Steel took to the sky once more, flying back toward the pod just in time to see a plasma blast tear a gaping hole in the famed globe atop the Daily Planet Building.

A jolt of anger shot through Superman. He watched as pieces of the Metropolis landmark crumbled to the ground. They were followed by the large steel letters that had spelled out the name of the great metropolitan newspaper that had served as Clark Kent's place of business and second home since his arrival in the city many years ago.

Infuriated, Superman reached the pod, unleashing two earth-shattering blows to the walker's midsection. Stunned, the creature fell back, toppling into the stone anchorage of the Metropolis bridge.

Landing atop his fallen adversary, the Man of Steel grabbed the pod's hull, tearing an opening in its thick metal skin. But before he could open a gash large enough for him to get at the alien's inner workings, the pod fired a plasma blast at Superman, who was now less than a foot from the source of the discharge.

FOOM!

The force of this latest blast catapulted Superman off the pod, sending him crashing through three buildings. He finally landed in the street, buried under tons of asphalt.

Lifting itself from the anchorage, the pod regained its footing, stepping back into the battle.

Swinging around for another pass, Batman guided the Batwing on a collision course with the alien walker. Firing off two additional missiles, the Dark Knight pulled hard on the controls, sending the Batwing into a steep climb, avoiding a series of plasma blasts. Looking down, though, Batman saw his latest barrage explode with no effect on the mechanical menace.

Snapper Carr had watched in shock as Superman took the full brunt of a point-blank blast. As with most people who grew up in Metropolis, Carr had worshiped the Man of Steel for as long as he could remember. As a kid, he had pretended to be Superman, pinning a bath towel around his neck, running around the house imagining he was flying.

When he grew up and became a reporter, one of Carr's first interviews was with his hero. Superman couldn't have been nicer, and Carr never forgot the kindness the great champion had shown him. The thought now that the protector of Metropolis had been defeated was almost more than he could bear. He had to do something, short of taking on the monster himself. He had to help Superman.

Carr raced through the devastation, searching for his fallen hero—not as a TV reporter, but as a citizen of this great city that had fallen under attack. Running in the direction in which he had seen Superman propelled, Carr soon found a crowd gathered around a mound of broken asphalt, heaving away chunks of what had once been the street. Carr jumped in, grabbing debris and flinging it off the mound.

When the pile was down to one final enormous slab, the helpers realized that even if they worked together, the piece was too big for them to move. Looking on helplessly, the crowd watched as the huge section, half the size of a football field, moved, slightly at first, then suddenly in one swift motion, lifting off, revealing Superman.

The Man of Steel looked shaken, but he had obviously recovered enough strength to hoist the heavy lid off his would-be tomb.

"Superman!" Carr cried. "Are you all right?"

Superman looked back at the pod, which was still blasting everything in its path. "Whatever that thing is," he groaned, pain and fatigue evident in his voice, "I've got to stop it."

Carr's face turned pale, his eyes opening wide in amazement. "Look!" he shouted, pointing at the asteroid several blocks away.

Superman and the others looked on in horror as the asteroid cracked open again and another pod emerged one leg at a time, each first stretching out, then planting itself on the ground. Finally, the body of the second pod came into view, followed by a third, which joined the others, unleashing plasma blasts among the fiery wreckage.

"It's not safe around here," Superman said to Carr. "Get out while I—"

At that moment, the now-familiar pain tore through Superman's skull. Clutching his head, collapsing to his knees, the Man of Steel screamed in agony as the latest flood of images ripped through his mind:

The sprawling wasteland of Mars.

Explosions in the desert.

The same military compound he had seen during the last psychic assault, this time filled with soldiers firing weapons.

A gleaming, high-tech research lab.

And the eyes, again the glowing orange eyes. Only this time a face emerged from the haze, a green-skinned face rising to a sharply pointed skull.

Finally, the meaning of the images that had plagued Superman for months crystallized in his mind. At last he knew where he had to go and what he needed to do.

Rising to his feet, the pain subsiding, Superman stared straight ahead.

"Are you okay?" Carr asked, waving his hand in front of Superman's glassy eyes. The Man of Steel remained motionless, unblinking. "Superman?"

Without a word, Superman rose into the sky, streaking into the distance, vanishing from view. His flight path took him right past the soaring Batwing.

Where's he going? Batman wondered, watching his friend disappear over the horizon.

Shaken from his thoughts by the deafening roar of jet engines, Batman looked out his window to see a squadron of Air Force fighter jets swooping toward the pods, firing missiles. Glancing to the street below, he also spotted tanks and jeeps carrying heavy ground artillery rolling toward the three walkers.

Speeding beside the rumbling tanks, bouncing along in his jeep, General Welles barked orders into his walkie-talkie, clearly in command of this operation. "Tactical seven!" he shouted. "Full frontal assault!"

Responding instantly, the tanks let loose with a blistering barrage of firepower.

Realizing there was nothing more he could do here, and glad the military had finally arrived, Batman banked the Batwing sharply to his right, zooming off in the direction he had seen Superman fly.

The image of Snapper Carr reporting live from downtown Metropolis filled television screens around the world. Walker pods could be seen over his shoulder, firing random blasts at a city that blazed all around them.

"After hours of intense battling, the heart of Metropolis lies in ruin," Carr reported as a plasma blast destroyed a tank behind him. "The military has arrived but seems unable to stop the deadly attacks.

"Meanwhile, we're getting reports that similar asteroids containing additional walker pods have landed all around the world, and more pods are arriving by the hour."

The news report went live to each scene of devastation. It showed explosions, craters, and pods in the desert around the pyramids in Egypt, and smoldering asteroids setting the lush jungle in Malaysia ablaze.

Returning to the image of Carr in Metropolis, the report wrapped up. "As the devastation continues," Carr said solemnly, "the question on everyone's lips is: Where is Superman?"

CHAPTER
4

Paradise Island in the Aegean Sea glimmered like a jewel, its perfect white-sand beaches shining in the warm sun, blue-green waves lapping gently on its shores. Home to the legendary Amazons—a race of women warriors created by the ancient gods—the beautiful island had always provided a refuge from their constant battles. Rising high from the center of the island, the fabled city of Themyscira served as a place of spiritual peace and intellectual pursuit for the many Amazons who called it home.

Two such women rode along the shore. The younger of the two, tall and strong, with long raven hair, reined in her powerful white horse, which whinnied, rearing up on its hind legs.

"Easy, girl," she said, reaching down and gently stroking the horse's neck. "Easy."

Next to her, atop a light brown horse, the older woman, regal and beautiful, with flowing blond hair, tightened the reins on her steed. She stared out to the sea.

"The omens we have heard tell of don't bode well, Mother," the younger woman commented, concern showing on her face. "It may be that mankind is facing its darkest hour."

The older woman frowned. "If that is the case, Diana," she began in a stern, domineering tone, "then mankind will have to face it alone." Pulling firmly on the reins, she turned her horse away from the water, back toward the great city.

"How can you say that?" Diana asked, frustration clear in her voice. It was true that her mother, the great Hippolyta, Queen of the Amazons, had far more experience in the ways of mortals than she did, but Diana still felt great worry for the humans of the outside world.

Pausing, Hippolyta turned back toward her daughter. "Whatever happens beyond these shores is not our concern," she stated impatiently. "Here, the gods will protect us." Then, turning back toward Themyscira, its gleaming palaces and ancient temples sparkling in the midday sun, Hippolyta rode back to the city.

Gazing from the sky out to the sea, then glancing back toward Themyscira, Diana pondered the fate of the humans, wondering how long her beloved city could stay free of the terrible troubles now besieging the mortal world.

"I hope you are right, Mother," she said sadly. Then, pulling her horse around, she followed the queen home.

Peering down from the cockpit of the Batwing, the Dark Knight was startled by the sight below. Having tracked Superman's flight path across the continent, he now approached a military base built into the side of the majestic Rocky Mountains in Colorado. The tall electrified fence that had surrounded the base lay shredded, strewn among the rocks. Overturned tanks, toppled guard towers, and flattened buildings covered the area between where the fence had stood and the sheer face of the mountain that housed the complex.

Sirens blared and red emergency lights flashed as the Batwing glided toward the entrance to the underground base, but there were no troops around to respond to the incursion. Once the plane touched down, its hydraulic cockpit canopy slid open, and Batman climbed from the craft, frowning as he closely surveyed the damage.

Two huge steel doors that had been built right into the mountainside lay crumpled on the ground, having apparently been torn off, leaving a gaping entryway to the vast complex beyond. Moving slowly, Batman cautiously stepped through the opening, venturing into the base's dark corridors.

Coming to a slightly opened door, the Dark Knight peeked into a room, where he discovered fifty to sixty hanging sacs identical to the ones he had seen at S.T.A.R. Labs. As he stepped into the room to investigate, a loud pounding from deep within the complex turned his attention away.

Following the repeated thuds through the maze of tunnels, Batman entered a large high-tech lab filled with rows of top-secret military hardware. At the far end of the lab he spotted Superman bashing on a thick steel door that resembled the entrance to an enormous bank vault.

Again and again the Man of Steel unleashed crushing blows with his powerful fists, each denting the massive door a bit further. Batman tossed a Batarang that zipped past Superman's head and lodged in the wall beside the door. The maneuver achieved the desired effect. Surprised, Superman stopped pounding and whirled to confront his friend.

"Hold it, Superman," said Batman, raising a gloved hand. "Destroying government property isn't your style. What's going on?"

"See for yourself," Superman replied, turning back to the dented door, grasping its edges. Grunting and straining from the enormous effort, Superman tore the door free and tossed it aside, where it landed with a thunderous clang.

Leading Batman through a control room filled with equipment panels, giant monitors, and computer consoles, Superman reached another sealed door at the far end of the room. This door, however, was far smaller than the first, and he easily ripped it from its hinges, revealing a vaultlike chamber bathed in eerie blue light.

Entering the chamber, Batman spied a tall green creature with long sticklike limbs, a thick plated chest, and a high pointed skull. Floating within a shimmering blue field of energy, the alien's arms, legs, and head were secured by large metal restraining cuffs.

"What is it?" Batman asked, staring at the strange being.

"Humankind's only hope," Superman replied cryptically, throwing a lever on a control console. The blue energy field vanished as the restraining cuffs retracted, allowing the alien to collapse in a heap. Superman stepped up quickly, catching the exhausted creature before he hit the floor.

"He's been trying to reach out to me telepathically for months," Superman explained, helping the alien to his feet. "But that stasis field in which he was trapped interfered with his psychic signals."

Batman recalled Superman's unexplained collapse at the radar substation.

"When his message finally broke through, I came here to rescue him," Superman finished as the alien regained his balance, slowly becoming able to stand under his own power.

"What's he doing here?" Batman asked suspiciously.

The alien looked right at the Dark Knight, his eyes glowing orange, his voice reverberating inside Batman's head.

"The alien invasion," said the telepathically transmitted voice. *"I came to warn you, but I was captured when I arrived on Earth and imprisoned here. Your government and soldiers wouldn't listen."*

"Big surprise," Batman said flatly, still staring at the alien.

"I sense you do not trust me," the alien said telepathically. *"Perhaps this will help."*

The two heroes watched in amazement as the alien underwent an astonishing transformation. His pointed skull rounded into a more familiar shape, his plated chest smoothed into that of a well-toned man, and his spindly arms and legs shortened and thickened, completing his overall human-like appearance. His skin remained green, his eyes orange. From his shoulders flowed a long blue cape, held in place by two yellow discs.

"I am J'onn J'onzz, also known as the Martian Manhunter," the alien said—aloud this time—extending his hand to Batman, who eyed him cautiously, not returning the gesture.

"Don't take it personally, J'onn," Superman said, smiling. "He doesn't trust anyone."

"A wise policy," J'onn said, lowering his hand and nodding toward Batman.

Superman led them back through the maze of corridors, and they soon emerged from the mountain. "We'll need to contact the Joint Chiefs right away," he said to Batman. "I'll fly on ahead. You take *him* in the Batwing."

"We're sure he's on *our* side?" Batman asked skeptically, suspicion growing in his mind. *This is, after all,* he thought, *an* alien *saying he warned us about an* alien *invasion.*

"I know we just met him," Superman replied. "But my instincts tell me to trust him. And right now, he's our only hope."

The Martian Manhunter stood silently. He had been met with nothing but distrust from the moment he arrived on Earth. He had no reason to expect anything else, even from the planet's greatest heroes.

Remaining on guard, Batman looked right at J'onn J'onzz. Nodding, he gestured toward the Batwing.

The overpowering glare of searchlights suddenly flooded the trio, momentarily blinding them.

"Stop right there, Superman!" barked a gruff voice.

A blazing light shone down from a hovering helicopter. Shielding his eyes, Superman saw a U.S. military officer at the head of a squadron of soldiers, their weapons aimed at the Man of Steel and his companions.

"You're trespassing in a restricted area," shouted the craggy-faced officer, a colonel from the markings on his uniform. "Our orders are to keep that freak here!"

"Wait!" Superman bellowed. "I'll vouch for him, Colonel. You must let us go."

"I don't think so," the colonel yelled back, his troops stepping closer to the threesome in the searchlights.

Batman noticed that the weapons carried by the soldiers were unlike any rifles he had ever seen—obviously not standard military issue.

"But the world's security may be at stake," Superman pointed out sternly.

A broad smile spread across the colonel's face as his men moved even closer. "That's why he'll never leave here alive," he said, signaling to his troops.

The colonel and his soldiers suddenly began to change, morphing from their human forms into monstrous aliens. They grew, their long torsos covered

with red, gray, and black patches, their enlarged
mouths glistening with needle-like teeth.

Those sacs I spotted must contain the real sol-
diers, Batman thought, the mystery becoming clear.
And the battle here was between those soldiers and
these aliens.

The three heroes braced themselves as the malevolent aliens quickly advanced.

A brilliant full moon filled the midnight sky over
Paradise Island with delicate, shimmering light, illuminating the royal palace of Themyscira. Its magnifi-
cent spires gleamed like gems against the lush
mountains that bordered the glorious city.

In contrast to its radiant exterior, the inner corridors of the palace were cloaked in darkness, broken
only by the flickering of candlelight from a series of
sconces protruding from the walls. A cloaked figure
made her way stealthily through the deserted halls,
cautious, silent, and unseen.

Reaching the enormous bronze doors in the main
hallway, the lone figure glanced back over her shoulder, then slowly opened the doors, slipping out into

the warm night. Crossing the palace grounds, her dark cloak pulled tight, she hurried across the city's main plaza, arriving quickly at the Temple of Athena, goddess of wisdom and military victory. Pausing one final time, glancing in all directions to make sure she was seen by no one, the furtive figure entered the temple.

Removing the hood of her cloak, Princess Diana walked briskly across the marble floor, stepping through shafts of moonlight that sliced between the temple's many huge columns. Diana knelt at the base of the massive statue of the goddess, looking up at the finely carved image.

Seeking counsel with Athena before going into battle was a long-standing tradition among Amazon warriors. Trained in the warrior ways of her people, Diana had been here many times, hoping for strength and guidance in a quest or a confrontation with an enemy of Themyscira. But she had never before sought out the blessing of Athena without her mother's knowledge or approval.

"Goddess," she began, "I know I seek your wisdom in a forthcoming battle not for the survival of the Amazons, or even in defense of the gods, but rather to assist the mortals of Earth. But, great Athena, I ask for your guidance and help in a task I consider just. The humans face their greatest challenge, and I fear that even their mightiest warriors cannot defeat the enemy who now attacks. The addition of my power may not be enough to turn the tide of battle, but my conscience screams out that I must at least try."

Lowering her head, Diana caught a glint of gold out of the corner of her eye. Glancing at a small pedestal across the room, she noticed a group of objects resting on the rounded stone platform.

"The Sacred Armor of the Amazons!" she cried, recognizing the hallowed relics. Realizing that this powerful armor could help her in her defense of the mortals, Diana also knew that its removal from the temple was forbidden.

Her mother would be furious. Diana struggled with her desire to do what she felt was right, weighing that against the possible consequences of violating both her mother's wishes and Amazon law.

Throwing off her cloak, Diana walked quickly across the temple. Reaching the pedestal, she lifted a red and gold breastplate and donned the armor. She next put on two silver bracelets and a gold tiara with a bright red star. Grasping the final item, a golden lasso, Princess Diana looked up once again at the statue.

"Mother and the Goddess, forgive me," she said, bowing. Then she turned and left the temple.

CHAPTER
5

Back at the military base in the heart of the Rocky Mountains, the heavily armed aliens drew closer to Superman, Batman, and J'onn J'onzz.

"It is them!" J'onn shouted, pointing at the hideous figures who now raised their gray and black weapons. "The invaders!"

The aliens opened fire, red beams of plasma energy flashing from their weapons, sending Batman and J'onn J'onzz diving for cover behind an overturned jeep. Stepping forward to confront the attackers, Superman was struck in the chest by an energy blast, sending him sprawling to the ground, facedown.

Behind the jeep, Batman pulled an exploding Batarang from his Utility Belt. "Stay down!" he shouted to J'onn, motioning for the Martian Man-hunter to remain low. Standing for a moment, energy beams streaking past his head, Batman tossed the Batarang into a cluster of aliens, then squatted back down beside J'onn.

KA-THOOM!

The Batarang detonated, scattering the aliens, fill-ing the area with dense black smoke.

Using the temporary cover, Batman stood again, searching for a more secure defensive position. An alien soldier slipped through the smoke, emerging several feet away, sneaking up behind Batman's back.

"Behind you!" J'onn shouted, leaping to his feet.

As Batman watched in amazement, J'onn J'onzz turned his body partially transparent. He stepped right through the Dark Knight, who spun around in time to see the Martian Manhunter release a blue en-ergy shield that radiated from his body just as the alien fired his weapon.

ZIIT-FOOM!

The energy beam was deflected by J'onn's shield, stopping the shot intended for Batman, knocking J'onn to the ground. Batman flung a Batarang at the attacker, stunning the alien, then rushed to the side of his fallen comrade.

"J'onn!" he shouted, realizing that there was more to this stranger than was instantly apparent. With one bold move he had displayed courage, loyalty, and an impressive array of powers. "Are you—"

"Injured?" J'onzz completed the question as Batman helped him to his feet. "Not seriously."

Nearby, Superman recovered from the energy blast and leapt into the air. Landing beside an overturned tank, the Man of Steel lifted the massive vehicle high over his head.

"Get J'onn to safety, Batman!" Superman shouted over the sound of a barrage of energy weapons firing at once. "I'll cover you!"

Superman hurled the massive tank at the alien army. It struck the ground with a sickening crunch, then skidded into the soldiers, toppling them like bowling pins, giving Batman and J'onn J'onzz time to race to the Batwing.

After helping J'onzz into the cockpit, Batman scrambled into the pilot's seat. "Hang on!" he shouted as the hydraulic canopy hissed shut. Glancing at the Martian Manhunter, he saw that J'onn's eyes glowed bright orange. "J'onn?" he called out, but received no answer. J'onzz appeared to be in a trance.

No time to waste, Batman thought, wondering what else there was to learn about his strange new companion. Frowning, he punched in the Batwing's ignition sequence, and its high-powered engine roared to life. Shoving the throttle forward, Batman blasted out of the complex, alien fire strafing the plane's heavily shielded hull.

When they were clear of the base, Batman glanced out the cockpit window to see Superman flying beside him. "That was close," Batman sighed, relieved to have escaped, though not really expecting a response from the zombie-like passenger in the seat behind him.

"We're not safe yet," J'onn J'onzz said flatly, pointing out the window. "Look."

A squadron of alien fighter jets zoomed from an underground cave, emerging from jagged cliffs among the mountains. The triangular fighters, covered in the all-too-familiar red, gray, and black pattern, flew in formation, closing in on the Batwing.

"Don't these guys have any other colors in their world?" Batman growled, peeling off in an evasive maneuver.

Ignoring Superman, the cluster of alien ships

followed Batman, matching the Batwing's dips and turns. Just as the lead fighter locked his weapon on the Batwing, Superman altered his course, flying right into the alien jet, slicing it in two.

The two halves of the severed fighter spun wildly out of control, one slamming into the side of a mountain, the other smashing into the fighter behind it, detonating a fiery explosion.

With the remainder of the squadron still tailing Batman, Superman swung around to take out a few more jets.

ZAP! ZAP! ZAP!

Unleashing a coordinated assault, the alien fighters blasted Superman repeatedly with their plasma beams, driving the Man of Steel into the mountainside. He dropped onto a narrow ledge, dazed from the impacts.

Using all his skill as a pilot, Batman weaved and turned, barely outpacing the pursuing fighters. Spotting a narrow passage between a series of jagged outcroppings, he pulled hard on the Batwing's steering control, aiming straight for the thin ribbon of space.

"Let's see them follow us through this," he said, his steely eyes focused on the path ahead. He skimmed close to the sharp, uneven peaks, barely avoiding them, swinging left, then right, navigating the slender maze, the difference between life and death a matter of inches.

But the aliens kept coming.

Exhibiting skillful piloting of their own, all but the last fighter in the squadron entered the maze successfully, shadowing the Batwing's every move. The last alien pilot flew too close to a craggy protrusion of rock, slamming into the side of the mountain and vaporizing in an orange fireball.

"They're still on us!" Batman growled, emerging from the thin slot between the mountains, looking for cover in the wide open valley below.

ZZZZZ-ATT!

An alien blast severed the Batwing's right stabilizer, shearing the winglike section off the plane's body and sending it tumbling to the gorge below. Flying now on one stabilizer, the Batwing spun hopelessly out of control. Unable to right the jet, Batman braced himself as the sharp rocks in the canyon below whirled toward him in a rush of inevitable destruction.

Seconds before impact, an eerie green glow flooded through the Batwing's cockpit window, bathing its two occupants in an unearthly emerald light. The plunging plane halted suddenly in midair, hovering inexplicably above the ground.

"What happened?" Batman asked, turning back to J'onn J'onzz.

J'onzz gestured toward the sky. "Help has arrived," he explained softly.

Peering out the window, Batman followed a green beam of energy leading from the circular aura that surrounded the Batwing to its source. The beam extended from a ring on the hand of a muscular, square-jawed man who hovered in midair. He was dressed in a green and black costume with the image of a lantern outlined in green on a white circle in the center of his chest.

"It is the warrior known as Green Lantern," J'onzz explained. "He is a member of the elite Green Lantern Corps, an intergalactic peacekeeping force. This particular Green Lantern, John Stewart, has shown exceptional courage and heroism in his defense of the galaxy."

"His timing is pretty good, too," Batman commented, still in awe of the incredible power displayed by his rescuer.

His muscles straining, Green Lantern maintained

his hold on the Batwing as an alien fighter jet swooped toward him, firing plasma blasts that the hero managed to just barely avoid.

"*Yiiiii!*" A battle cry shrieked from above the Batwing.

Something with wings soared past the plane as it hung suspended in Green Lantern's power beam. *A bird?* Batman thought for an instant. *No, a person... with wings?*

The figure in the sky—a petite woman with long, body-length wings and feathers covering her head extending up in two yellow points—carried a mace. Reaching the attacking alien fighter, she swung the mace in a wide arc. Jagged bolts of white, sizzling energy crackled from the head of the mace, increasing its force enormously.

THOOM!

With one swift blow, the winged warrior destroyed the alien jet. Its flaming wreckage plummeted to the canyon below.

Batman recognized the figure in the sky as she struck another blow, exploding a second fighter.

"Hawkgirl!" Batman cried, turning to J'onn. The Dark Knight had teamed up before with the hero known on Earth as Hawkgirl. She was called Shayera

Hol on her native planet of Thanagar. There, her phenomenal powers of observation made her a superb undercover detective. The diminutive yet powerful warrior impressed even the Darkknight Detective with her skills. At the moment, however, her abilities wielding the mace were much more in demand. "What's she doing here?"

Ignoring Batman's question, J'onn J'onzz once again became partially transparent. He rose from his seat, passing through the Batwing's canopy, joining Hawkgirl and Green Lantern in the sky as Batman looked on in astonishment.

Green Lantern gently placed the damaged Batwing onto a smooth outcropping just as another alien fighter swooped toward the trio in the sky, its weapons blazing. Scattering in three directions, the heroes avoided the blasts; then a red and blue figure streaked through the air, exploding through the fighter, demolishing it.

Superman, fully recovered, slowed to a stop, hovering in the sky next to the others. "Good to see you, John," he said to Green Lantern. "Where have you been?"

"Sorry I'm late," Green Lantern replied. "I had to handle an uprising near Rigel-Nine." As the Green

Lantern for an entire quadrant of the galaxy—which just happened to include the solar system containing Earth—John Stewart's responsibilities often took him far from his home planet.

Superman nodded. Although he was known as a protector of Earth, the Man of Steel had often been involved in conflicts on other worlds. He was well acquainted with galactic responsibility.

The four heroes flew toward the next wave of alien fighters. Superman grabbed a fighter by its wing, spun it around and around, then released it, sending the jet slamming into the side of a cliff, where it shattered.

Hawkgirl continued to devastate fighters with her energy-enhanced mace, knocking the tail off one, splitting another in half.

Nearby, Green Lantern concentrated a tight beam of energy from his ring, striking a zooming fighter and blowing it to bits.

Meanwhile, J'onn J'onzz hovered in midair, setting himself up as an easy target. When an alien fighter fired at him, J'onn made himself semitransparent, allowing the blast to pass right through him and strike another alien jet.

KA-THOOM!

Pieces of the jet scattered against the mountain cliffs. On the outcropping, Batman scrambled from the Batwing, diving for cover just as a flaming piece of debris from the ship slammed into the ground next to his plane. Glancing up, he saw another fighter catch Hawkgirl with a blast, sending her tumbling down onto a small plateau.

Hawkgirl struggled to her feet, then collapsed from the effort.

As the fighter swung around to finish off its helpless target, a red and gold form streaked down from the sky, landing in front of Hawkgirl.

"Allow me," said Princess Diana of Themyscira, standing tall, raising her arms as the alien ship let loose a series of blasts aimed at the defenseless, winged young woman.

Using her silver bracelets, Diana deflected the searing energy beams one by one. The ancient armor was empowered by the goddess Athena and was resistant to all force. Maintaining a collision course with Diana, the ship drew near, firing nonstop.

SKRING! SKRING! SKRING!

A round of plasma blasts bounced off Diana's bracelets, ricocheting back to the ship.

THOOM!

Their own deadly weapons tore through the alien ship, demolishing it, but the flaming chunks that remained plunged toward Hawkgirl and Diana. The princess knew she could fly from the ledge to safety, but there simply wasn't enough time to rescue the helpless hero sprawled beside her.

With the plummeting fuselage mere yards from her head, Diana looked up in great surprise as a transparent, green-tinted bubble suddenly appeared around the ledge on which she stood. The smoldering wreckage slammed into the emerald dome, exploding harmlessly. Peering through the dome, Diana saw Green Lantern hovering above. A power beam from his ring had formed the protective shield.

Superman flew up alongside Green Lantern, an alien fighter jet firmly gripped in his hands.

"Who's the rookie in the tiara?" Green Lantern asked the Man of Steel, nodding toward Diana.

"I'm not sure," Superman grunted, tossing the final alien plane at the mountain's face, where it exploded in flames.

The battle was over. All the attacking alien fighters had been destroyed. The group of heroes, most of whom had never met before, had just worked together as a team—a very effective team. This fact was not lost on the Man of Steel.

"Thanks for showing up when you did," Hawkgirl said as Princess Diana helped the winged warrior to her feet. The two took to the air to join Superman, Green Lantern, and J'onn J'onzz.

Hovering in the sky, the group of flying heroes peered down at their handiwork—the scattered remains of wrecked alien fighters.

On an outcropping below, Batman looked up at the others just as a streaking red blur came speeding up next to him.

"Hey, Bats, you dropped this," said the Flash, stopping next to Batman, handing him the sheared-off stabilizer from the Batwing. "I found it on my way here."

Landing one by one, the other heroes joined Batman and Flash on the ledge.

"I trust you were not injured," Diana said to Batman.

Flash's eyes opened wide at the sight of the princess. The youngest of the group, Wally West, known to the world as the Flash, thought of himself as a ladies' man despite his total lack of experience. Impulsive, the Flash often spoke first and thought later.

"Whoa!" he exclaimed, looking at Diana and smiling. "Where have you been all my life?"

Having no experience with humans—particularly young, brash, cocky ones—the princess took his question literally. "Themyscira," she replied matter-of-factly.

"Huh?" Flash said, scratching his head.

"Themyscira is the home of the Amazons," Hawkgirl explained, astonishment apparent in her voice. "But I always thought it was merely a legend."

"I assure you, it's as real as the ground on which we stand," Diana said proudly. "I am Diana, Princess of the Amazons. I am also called Wonder Woman by many."

"No wonder," Flash said, grinning broadly. "Pinch me, I must be dreaming."

Superman, who stood next to Flash, jabbed him gently in the ribs.

"Ow!" Flash yelped, rubbing his side, the smile vanishing from his face.

Wonder Woman continued: "Themyscira is protected by the gods. Though others of my kind chose to ignore the troubles mankind now faces, I could not idly stand by while the rest of the world was in danger."

"It was lucky you showed up when you did," Superman pointed out.

"No," J'onn J'onzz said, shaking his head. "Not luck. I telepathically summoned all of these heroes."

Flash rubbed the back of his neck, shaking his head rapidly. "Look," he began. "I'm usually pretty quick on the uptake, but would someone please tell me what the heck is going on here?"

Superman, Batman, and J'onn J'onzz immediately turned to one another, exchanging glances, eyebrows raised, wondering where to begin.

"I think I can explain," Superman finally said, stepping forward. As he filled the newcomers in on the details of the alien invasion, the telepathic messages, and the rescue of J'onn J'onzz, the Man of Steel used his heat vision to weld the Batwing's severed stabilizer back onto the aircraft. When he finished, the others still looked puzzled.

Wonder Woman spoke first. Though she was no stranger to battle, this tale of alien attack, human devastation, and the arrival of a messenger from Mars was unlike any she had ever heard.

"So, J'onn J'onzz, you came from Mars to warn us?" she asked, making sure she had understood Superman's tale.

"This is too weird," Flash said, throwing up his hands before J'onn could reply to Wonder Woman's question. Used to straightforward contests of strength, power, and, of course, speed, he had rarely encountered anyone or anything he couldn't defeat or outrun. But he simply couldn't get his mind around the enormous scale of the threat Earth now faced.

"I've seen stranger things," Green Lantern offered, himself a veteran of countless galactic conflicts. Turning to J'onn J'onzz, he asked, "What exactly can you tell us about these invaders?"

All eyes focused on the Martian, who sighed deeply.

"We first encountered the invaders one thousand of your Earth years ago. It was a Golden Age on Mars. Our civilization was at the height of its peace and prosperity. War, poverty, and hunger had been eliminated. Architecture, literature, music, art, and philosophy flourished. Great Martian cities rose across the planet, culture thrived, productivity soared, and all citizens studied self-improvement as a way of life."

The others all listened raptly, visions of a planet-wide paradise filling their heads.

"But our Golden Age ended abruptly," J'onn J'onzz continued, "the day *they* arrived. I still don't know where they came from, but I will never forget that day. Streaking asteroids tore through the sky, slamming into our cities and creating huge craters. The craters then released their huge walker pods, which fired plasma blasts, obliterating everything in their paths. At first they only destroyed our buildings and creations, but eventually, our entire way of life was ruined.

"We Martians were a peaceful people, having ended war on our planet hundreds of years earlier. The taking of any life was abhorrent to us, but our only option was to quickly relearn the ways of war.

"Amid the smoldering ruins of our once-great civilization, we resorted to guerrilla tactics. We tossed high-impact firebombs at one or two walkers at a time, engulfing them in flames, bringing them down.

"Though Mars was momentarily triumphant, more walkers inevitably came, raining widespread destruction. Any chance of saving our world slipped from our grasp.

"The battles raged on for centuries. With each small victory came even greater setbacks. Finally, every trace of what we had built over thousands of years was obliterated. Although we fought valiantly, the invaders were parasites who fed on our psychic energy. When they touched us, our very life force was transferred to their bodies. Then they suspended our near-dead bodies in fluid inside larval sacs, in a state that was not quite death, but not truly life either. There we would stay forever.

"As we grew weaker from this psychic transfer, they grew stronger. They even absorbed our shape-changing abilities, altered their appearance to look like us, infiltrated our guerrilla operations, and destroyed us from within.

"Finally, a small group of Martian survivors, of which I was one, planned a last, desperate attack. Wearing gas masks, we stormed the invaders' underground stronghold, which they had established deep beneath the Martian surface. After battling our way past their guards, we lobbed gas grenades throughout the complex, unleashing a powerful nerve gas that paralyzed them. The sickly purple gas spread to every corner of the underground stronghold.

"Invaders collapsed to the ground everywhere, paralyzed by the gas, though many fought back right up until their final moment of consciousness. The attack was ultimately successful, but the cost was dear.

When the thick purple clouds dissipated, I stood alone in the complex, my comrades strewn in lifeless heaps around my feet.

"I was the only survivor, the last of my kind."

J'onn J'onzz paused, overcome by the memory. He had never told this tale to anyone, and sharing it now brought back all the horrors of that day so long ago. He felt as if it had just occurred.

The others remained silent, their heads bowed respectfully, no one knowing what to say or if saying anything was appropriate.

J'onn recovered his composure and broke the silence for the grateful group. "Alone, I sealed up their underground citadel to keep them in a constant state of suspended animation, locking them in the stronghold behind two enormous doors. I then carved Martian symbols onto the doors, telling the tale of what occurred, recording it for all time, should anyone care to know. As long as the chamber remained sealed, with no new air entering, the effects of the gas would continue indefinitely.

"For more than five hundred years I stood guard over them, making sure this horrendous evil never escaped."

The others exchanged quick looks of amazement. *How old is J'onn J'onzz?* they all wondered, but they remained silent.

"But then, while I was in a hibernation cycle, astronauts from Earth unsealed the stronghold and accidentally revived the invaders."

"Wait a second," Flash interrupted. "I remember reading about that mission. They never said anything about finding life on Mars."

"Some pencil pusher in Washington probably decided it should be classified information," Green Lantern explained, scowling with disdain.

"With all the Martians gone, the awakened invaders had nothing to feed upon," J'onn J'onzz continued. "So they turned their sights to Earth. I narrowly escaped, and came here first to warn the humans of the coming danger. Unfortunately, I was met with fear and distrust, and immediately placed into the stasis field from which Superman rescued me, before anyone here on Earth could listen to my story.

"While I was being held against my will, the invaders sent advance agents here to disable Earth's defenses."

Batman's face tightened into a grimace. "That's why they sabotaged the deep-space monitoring network," he said, the pieces falling into place. The mystery he had been pursuing for many months was finally solved. "And that's why they destroyed the radar dish. So we couldn't detect their activities or have any warning of their approaching invasion."

"Yes," J'onn replied, nodding slowly. "And to make sure I couldn't escape or attempt to stop them, they even took over the military base where I was being held, using the shapeshifting power they stole from my people to morph into likenesses of the soldiers. No doubt the real soldiers are hanging in larval sacs somewhere inside that base."

"I saw them," Batman reported, flashing on the gruesome scene he had encountered upon first entering the mountain complex.

"It took all of my mental power to overcome the stasis field and contact you," J'onn J'onzz said, turning to Superman, concluding his astonishing tale.

Eyes smoldering with rage, fists clenched tightly, Green Lantern stepped forward. "We've got to stop them before it's too late!" he announced, stepping up as the group's leader. With his experience in the Green Lantern Corps, he was comfortable commanding others, and he naturally assumed the role of leader would be his on this mission.

J'onn J'onzz looked at Green Lantern sadly, the horror of his tale still fresh in his mind. "It may already be too late," he said softly.

CHAPTER 6

As the heroes discussed their next moves, the aliens continued to arrive, wreaking devastation around the globe.

In Metropolis, huge sections of the city lay in ruins, with no end to the assault in sight. Standing amid the destruction, Snapper Carr reported live to an increasingly anxious audience around the world.

"This is Snapper Carr live from downtown Metropolis," he began. Behind him, the terrifying blasts from three alien walker pods still crashing through the rubble punctuated his even-toned commentary. "As you can see, alien walkers continue clearing the area around the impact site." He gestured to the long trench carved by the asteroid's impact.

Nearby, General Welles barked orders to his troops, who continued the nearly hopeless attempt to stop the destruction. Stepping up to the general, Carr pointed to the camera, then began an impromptu interview. "General Welles!" he shouted, to be heard over the alien plasma blasts. "Our military seems unable to stop them. Why?"

Welles turned his large, weary face to the camera. "All our big missiles have been disarmed," he barked angrily. "And our self-proclaimed protector, Superman, who disarmed those missiles in the first place, has apparently abandoned us."

Having gotten his tasty sound bite, Carr stepped away from the general as the camera zoomed in for a close-up of the reporter's face. "Earlier, Senator J. Allen Carter had this to say."

At an unseen signal from Carr, the engineers back in the studio ran a tape of Senator Carter. Standing at a lectern in a room crowded with reporters, Carter spoke slowly and calmly.

"When I first proposed my peace initiative, no one ever imagined we would face an invasion like this," he began. "Now, we must stand together and resist this aggression."

The tape ended, and the TV image cut seamlessly back to Carr.

"Those comments from Senator J. Allen—"

A horrendous noise from behind stopped Carr mid-sentence. Turning, he saw the huge alien asteroid shaking and splitting down the middle.

"Wait!" he shouted, stepping instinctively away from the asteroid, his cameraman sticking with his every move. "We have a breaking development. The asteroid that carried the devastating walkers is moving again. New cracks appear to be forming."

KA-RAKKK!

The asteroid was splitting open like an enormous egg. The two halves fell away, revealing thick black smokestacks reaching into the sky, like the antennae of some monstrous being.

"Oh, my lord!" General Welles gasped, watching as the smokestacks rose higher and higher.

Snapper Carr dashed for cover, his cameraman capturing images of the ever-growing menace.

Behind the smokestacks, a massive machine emerged, looking like both a living organism and a mechanical construct. Two heartlike chambers on the device's exterior pulsated in alternating pumping rhythms, flashing like two malevolent red eyes. A spinning drill dropped from the side of the machine, splitting the asphalt, digging down into the Earth.

Building in intensity from deep within the machine, black clouds spewed from the smokestacks, filling the sky with darkness, blocking out the sun.

On the cliffs of the Rocky Mountains, half a continent away, the heroes heard a deep rumbling. They watched in horror as unnatural darkness covered the distant sky and shafts of lightning crackled from the haze, dancing on the horizon.

"What is that?" Wonder Woman asked. All eyes focused on the approaching maelstrom. "It is like no storm I have ever witnessed."

J'onn J'onzz stared at the darkening sky, knowing its significance all too well. "It has begun," he announced as the black clouds spread like a visible evil.

"What are they doing?" Hawkgirl asked, understanding from J'onn's tone that this was no natural phenomenon, but rather the horrific handiwork of the aliens.

"The invaders are nocturnal," J'onn explained.

"They want to block out the sun so they can live in perpetual darkness."

Flash turned to Batman. "Friends of yours?" he asked, winking.

"This is no joke," Batman replied tersely, rarely amused even in the best of times.

Finding all this seriousness oppressive, Flash turned to J'onn J'onzz. "What's the big problem?" he asked, shrugging. "Can't you just whip up another batch of that nerve gas?"

"Unfortunately, no," J'onn replied, shaking his head. "The gas can only be made from a rare Martian plant. I brought a sample with me, but it was destroyed when I was captured."

Flash's expression soured. "Uh, what's plan B?"

"The invaders have set up a series of interconnected underground ionization factories around the planet," J'onn J'onzz explained, "each producing the black ion clouds you see in the sky. It is the next phase in their plan to conquer Earth."

"Then we'll have to take out those factories," Wonder Woman said confidently.

Green Lantern turned abruptly, standing face to face with the Amazon Princess. "Lady, this is no job for amateurs," he snarled derisively.

Wonder Woman met his gaze unflinchingly, stepping closer to the emerald-clad galactic defender. "We Amazons are born warriors," she snapped back. "Want to test me?"

Superman stepped between the two heroes before any blows were exchanged. "Let's not fight among ourselves," he said in a soft conciliatory voice. Grabbing Green Lantern by the arm, the Man of Steel pulled him aside. "John, we're going to need all the help we can get," he said firmly.

"Fine," Green Lantern replied, not sounding entirely convinced. "I'm sorry, *Your Highness*," he said to Wonder Woman, using the royal address sarcastically.

So this is how I am judged in the world of mortals? Diana thought, rage building inside her. Clenching her fists, lips pursed, she stepped back, swallowing her anger for the good of the group.

Sensing a victory of sorts, Green Lantern assumed his leadership role once more. "Tactically, we'll have multiple objectives," he announced, turning to face the others. "So we'll need to split into teams."

In the blink of an eye, Flash appeared next to Wonder Woman, placing his arm around her shoulder. "Dibs on the Amazon," he said, unfurling a big grin.

"What?" Diana shouted. Still fuming from her confrontation with Green Lantern, she removed Flash's arm from her shoulder forcefully, glaring at the Scarlet Speedster. *Am I some prize to be won?* she wondered, confusion mixing with her anger.

Dividing the group into teams for maximum efficiency, Green Lantern sent Batman, Wonder Woman, and J'onn J'onzz to Egypt to take out a factory beneath the desert. Superman and Hawkgirl returned to Metropolis to deal with the factory there. Taking Flash as his partner, Green Lantern headed for the jungles of Malaysia to dismantle the ion factory that had been set up in the rain forest.

Flying across the ocean, surrounded by a green energy field propelled by the awesome force of his power ring, Green Lantern sped toward Malaysia, hovering several yards above the churning sea.

Beside him, the Fastest Man Alive raced across the ocean, running on its surface. A ten-foot-tall wall of water, churned up by his incredibly fast feet, sprayed out behind him.

The Flash turned to his partner, who struggled to keep up, soaring through the air just above him. "You're no fun!" he said, pouting. "Why couldn't I go with the Amazon Princess? I really think she was beginning to like me."

Green Lantern shook his head at the blind confidence—more like blissful ignorance—of the young hero racing along the ocean's surface. "This isn't supposed to be fun." He shouted to be heard over the roar of the wake rising behind the Scarlet Speedster. "We've got a job to do, and we'll do it better without distractions. Understood?"

"Yeah, yeah," Flash sighed, realizing that Green Lantern was right, even though he didn't like it. "I understand. No distractions."

Slowing as they approached the shoreline, the speeding swaths of emerald and crimson reached the beach, then headed deep into the dense Malaysian jungle. Reaching a cliff overlooking a clearing, the heroes peered down at the huge alien ion factory.

The massive structure, so completely out of place in the center of a pristine jungle, rose to the sky like an enormous mutated insect. Curved walls led to two glowing, pulsating chambers that flashed with red light, pumping ionic energy from deep below the Earth's surface. A spinning drill violated the once-lush jungle floor, now charred and shredded, and soaring smokestacks belched black clouds of ionic fumes into the darkening sky. Alien walkers surrounding the factory blasted the thick jungle foliage, leveling ancient trees.

"That's our target," Green Lantern announced, pointing to the devastation below. "Now, listen up. Here's our plan."

"What plan?" Flash replied impatiently, shrugging his shoulders and scowling. "We go in, we kick their butts, we leave, right? So let's get this over with."

Before Green Lantern could reply, Flash took off, running straight down the sheer face of the cliff, dashing toward the factory. Surrounded by a dust cloud kicked up by Flash's hasty departure, the Emerald Warrior sighed, shaking his head at the boy's recklessness.

Arriving at the edge of the clearing, Flash halted abruptly, then whistled at the walkers, waving his arms and shouting, "Hey, over here!"

Having garnered their attention, Flash streaked among the walkers, using his speed to easily avoid their repeated plasma blasts. "Ha, ha! Missed me!" he cried as the aliens fired at the spot where Flash had been standing and taunting them just milliseconds earlier.

Brimming with confidence once again, working his

way to the outer walls of the factory, Flash tripped over a defensive mine sensitive enough to be triggered even by his slight footfall.

THOOSSHH!

Propelled high into the air, Flash rode a sloshing wave of a thick gluelike material. "Whoa!" he cried, falling back to the ground, covered in the gelatinous goo.

Watching from the cliff, Green Lantern shook his head. "Fool!" he cried, powering up his ring.

Landing on the ground in a pool of the sticky substance, Flash struggled in vain to free himself, his arms and legs firmly stuck. Looking up, he spotted a walker pod lumbering toward him. A blast from the pod seared the glue just inches from his leg. The enormous walker rotated, its plasma cannon taking dead aim on the trapped figure in red.

A green beam slashed through the air, slicing off one of the walker's legs. "Hang tight, hotshot!" Green Lantern shouted as he soared above.

Thrown off balance by the loss of its leg, the pod staggered, stumbled, then finally toppled to the ground, shattering to bits on the jungle floor.

Hovering above Flash, Green Lantern looked down at the pathetic sight in the puddle of goo.

"Hey!" Flash said casually, as if running into his friend on a street corner. "I'm sorta stuck here," he added, nodding at the pool surrounding him.

"So I see," Green Lantern replied, looking back and spotting two more walkers heading toward them. "Of all the idiotic, boneheaded, glory-grabbing moves! Haven't you ever heard of teamwork?" Using the beam from his power ring as a laser, he sliced through the sticky goo, releasing Flash's arms and legs.

ZZAATT!

As Flash leapt free, a plasma blast split the ground where he had been trapped. "Uh, maybe we'd better save the motivational speeches till later," he suggested as the walker fired another blast at the heroes.

Expanding the dimension of the energy beam from his ring, Green Lantern widened the thin shaft of light into a protective shield.

THOOM!

The next blast erupted against the translucent green dome, dissipating around the heroes. Shifting its strategy, the walker detonated a grenade, releasing a sickly gas that penetrated the green shield.

Vulnerable to the noxious fumes, Green Lantern collapsed to the ground, choking.

Racing to his friend's side, Flash swung his arms in circles like two high-powered fan blades, his elbows locked. As his arms spun faster and faster, a whirlwind whipped up, blowing away the toxic gas.

When the air cleared, Flash looked up to see two walkers towering directly over him, their plasma weapons ready.

"Uh-oh," he said weakly. "Gotta run."

Scooping his fallen partner into his arms, the Scarlet Speedster streaked into the nearby thicket, vanishing from view just as the walkers opened fire.

Recovering from the effects of the gas, Green Lantern raised his head to look up at his partner. "I hope the others are having better luck than we are," he groaned as Flash carried him deep into the jungle.

CHAPTER
7

The great pyramids of Egypt rose from an endless expanse of desert. Swirling gusts of wind catapulted sand through the air, sending it cascading along the sides of these towers of old. Nearby, the mighty Sphinx sat as it had for thousands of years, a silent sentry, witness to an endless stream of travelers, visitors, and most recently, hostile alien invaders.

In the wide stretch of sand around these marvels of the ancient world, another alien ionization factory sprawled like a cancerous growth, pounding and drilling, vibrating with energy, its towering smokestacks spewing black filth into the air.

Crouching in the shadows at the base of the Sphinx, Batman and Wonder Woman waited, he more patiently than she. Peering out, his dark cowl glinting briefly in the last ray of sunlight breaking through the thickening black clouds, Batman spotted a walker patrolling nearby. Ducking back to the safety of the shadows, he signaled for Diana to remain still.

"Hiding like cowards is not the Amazon way," she protested when the walker had tromped past. Rising from her squatting position, Wonder Woman stepped forward. Batman moved swiftly, standing and blocking her path.

"Not yet," he said, always the cautious warrior, preferring stealth to hasty, grand gestures. "They must have a weakness. When we find it, then we'll strike."

Rising from the sand like a slender green ghost, J'onn J'onzz appeared before the Dark Knight and the Amazon Princess, his semitransparent form solidifying before their eyes. Batman, for one, was still not used to these unexpected appearances, and he wondered once again about the full extent of his new comrade's abilities.

"I have scouted the outer walls of the factory," J'onn reported, joining the others in the shadows. "There are no openings."

This was more than Wonder Woman could bear.

During her years battling alongside her fellow Amazons, she had feared no one and nothing, rushing into battle, knowing the gods supported her efforts. All this sneaking about and lurking in shadows was repellent to her warrior's soul.

"If there are no openings," she began, standing up, springing from her hiding spot, "then we'll make our own!"

J'onn J'onzz turned to stop her, but Batman grasped his arm firmly, holding him back.

"Wait!" the Dark Knight said, realizing that keeping Diana silent and still for much longer would not be easy. "Let's see what she can do." J'onn nodded in agreement.

Taking to the air, the Amazon Princess soared above a walker keeping watch near the factory. Unfurling her Golden Lasso as she dodged a blast from a plasma cannon, Wonder Woman dove toward the walker's legs.

Tossing the gleaming rope, Diana looped the lasso around all three of the pod's tall legs, pulling it taut. After flying around the walker several times, she landed. "Hera, give me strength!" she shouted, invoking the name of the queen of the gods.

Pulling with all her great might, Wonder Woman tightened the lasso around the walker's legs. Attempting to step, the giant pod teetered, its balance destroyed by the tightly drawn lasso. Tipping over, the walker crashed into an outer wall of the ion factory, tearing open a gaping hole in its side.

From their hiding place, Batman and J'onn J'onzz exchanged looks of amazement, then watched as the dust cleared, revealing Wonder Woman standing atop the fallen walker, pointing proudly into the large hole she had created with her strength and cunning. "There's your opening," she announced.

"Not bad," Batman commented to J'onn as Diana flew through the opening. They hurried in after her.

Stepping into the factory, Batman noticed immediately that the dark corridor had a damp, almost organic feel, as if they had entered the body of a huge living creature rather than a building. He spotted a troop of aliens, armed with the same type of plasma rifles he had encountered at the military base where they had found J'onn. The aliens retreated, turning to fire every few steps.

Leaping forward, Wonder Woman deflected the blasts with her silver bracelets. "They run like cowards!" she shouted back to the others. "What are you waiting for?"

Rushing ahead, followed closely by J'onn J'onzz, Diana pursued the aliens, who raced deeper into the dark recesses of the factory, carefully avoiding the pools of sunlight pouring in through the hole in the outer wall.

Ever the detective, Batman paused, looking up at the shafts of light streaming in, his eyes narrowing, his mind processing various details of the entire affair. Then he turned and ran deeper into the factory, hurrying to catch up with his comrades.

Superman looked out on his beloved city of Metropolis, now lying in flaming ruins. His concern for the fate of the planet consumed his every thought, but his heart ached for his adopted home in a special, more personal way. He felt for this great city, brought to its knees by the blight of alien invasion.

Hawkgirl pounded a walker pod with her energized mace, shredding it into metallic slivers. Then she flew toward another approaching alien.

Superman, meanwhile, grabbed a pod by the leg,

tearing the bottom half of the mechanical limb from its joint. He hurled it like a spear at the ion factory.

SCHWIPP!

The projectile pierced the factory's outer wall, cleaving an opening.

"Hawkgirl! Follow me!" Superman cried, flying through the hole into the factory. Within seconds Hawkgirl landed beside him. As they explored the mazelike interior of the structure, it occurred to Superman that it looked more like the bones and tissues of a living organism than the steel and glass of a factory complex.

"Keep a sharp eye out," Superman warned Hawkgirl.

"I always do," she replied, using her keen sight to scan the passageway ahead.

ZING! ZING! ZING!

Alien blaster fire rained down all around them from an outcropping above. Superman spotted a squadron of aliens rushing toward them, weapons blazing.

"Stay back!" he yelled. "I'll—"

Hawkgirl rushed past Superman, ignoring his plea, flying right into the cluster of eight heavily armed aliens.

"Yiiiii!" she bellowed, shouting a traditional battle cry from her home world of Thanagar as she engaged the enemies, ferociously swinging her mace. White bolts of energy sprang from its head as the powerful weapon slammed into the first two aliens, taking them out instantly.

Dodging their weapons' fire, Hawkgirl backhanded three more, one of whom came flying right at Superman. Ducking, the Man of Steel turned to see the alien splat against the wall behind him, dripping down the slick surface like melting ice cream.

"Whoa," Superman muttered, astonished and impressed by his teammate's prowess. Turning back to the battle, he saw that it was over. Hawkgirl stood beside the final three vanquished aliens. He stared in disbelief.

"What?" Hawkgirl said defensively, noticing his look of amazement. "There's a time for words and a time for action. I knew if we hesitated, they would have had the opportunity to gain the upper hand, and I simply could not allow that." Then she took to the air, flying deeper into the factory.

Superman followed Hawkgirl, and the two flew together through the narrow hallways of the complex maze.

"They're close by," Hawkgirl announced excitedly, rounding a sharp curve. "I can almost smell them."

"Are you always so eager to fight?" Superman asked, somewhat repulsed by his partner's savagery, yet very glad they were on the same side.

"My home planet, Thanagar, is a warlike world," Hawkgirl explained. "There, one must strike first or die."

Just then, plasma blasts ricocheted off the wall above the heroes' heads. They halted and turned to give chase, with Hawkgirl in the lead.

Unlike the previous assault, this time the aliens fled, apparently unwilling to confront the winged warrior again. As Hawkgirl pursued them down a constricted corridor, a wall—more like an organic membrane than a manufactured structure—closed between her and the retreating attackers.

Whirling around, Superman spied another membrane closing behind him, like the pupil of an eye dilating in bright light. "It's a trap!" he shouted as two more walls slammed shut, forming a tiny chamber around the two heroes.

The telltale hiss of gas pouring into the sealed area alerted Superman to the final piece of the plan. Hawkgirl fell to the ground, choking, coughing violently, and gasping for breath.

"Hang on, Hawkgirl," Superman shouted, latching onto the wall behind him, pulling powerfully, trying to open the membrane.

ZZZAAATT!!

Searing jolts of electric energy shot into the Man of Steel's hands, forcing him to release his grip. Stunned, he collapsed to the ground beside Hawkgirl as the thick, noxious fumes filled the airtight chamber.

Deep beneath the Egyptian desert, Batman, Wonder Woman, and J'onn J'onzz were caught in a barrage of alien fire. As the others desperately sought a way out, Wonder Woman deflected incoming plasma blasts with her bracelets.

"They've blocked our path again!" she shouted, glancing around for a tunnel or corridor leading away from the alien troops.

"It's almost as if they know what we're thinking," Batman added while pulling an exploding Batarang from his Utility Belt and tossing it at the soldiers.

THOOM!

The Batarang detonated, scattering the attackers

momentarily. He had bought the group a few seconds.

"Any ideas, J'onn?" Batman asked his teammate.

J'onn J'onzz stood motionless and silent, as if in a trance, his large eyes glowing orange.

"J'onn?" Batman repeated.

The glow in his eyes fading, the Martian Manhunter withdrew from his trance and turned to Batman. "Superman and Hawkgirl are down," he stated sadly. "They have failed."

"What?" Diana asked in disbelief, wondering how he could possibly know. "Are you sure?"

J'onn nodded with certainty. "I can sense it," he said softly. His eyes suddenly opened wide and a tense expression washed over his calm face, as if he was hearing something the others could not. "This way!" he said quickly, pointing down a corridor to their right. "Hurry!"

With the others following closely, J'onn led the way into a tiny side passageway just as three walls slammed shut in the corridor they had left. "Had we stayed a moment longer, we would have been trapped in the same manner as Superman and Hawkgirl," J'onn explained, gesturing to the sealed membranes.

"These factories react like living beings, anticipating our moves, attempting to outwit and trap us. Quickly now, follow me!"

Wonder Woman and the Martian Manhunter took to the air, flying through a small hole at the top of a side wall. Batman followed, firing a grappling Batarang into the ceiling, then pulling himself up and through the same hole. Pausing and looking back, the three heroes saw that they were alone.

"We lost them," Wonder Woman announced.

"For the moment," Batman added.

"Look," J'onn said, pointing ahead, leading the others to the end of a long corridor that opened into a huge cavern. "It's the central core. The heart of the entire global factory complex."

Batman and Wonder Woman gazed at the central core, a deep pulsing sound filling their ears. Large organic-looking pumps throbbed in sequence like pounding hearts. Energy pulsed through miles of tangled, veinlike pipes as hundreds of alien technicians monitored the complex system.

"This is the engine that manufactures the ion energy, powering the complex, creating the black clouds above," J'onn explained. "It all begins here."

Glancing around, trying to get a handle on all this alien technology, Batman's mind raced for a solution. "How can we shut it down?" he asked.

J'onn pointed to a large glowing crystal in the center of the complex. Black energy surged through its multifaceted, irregular configuration. "The Ion Matrix Crystal is the power source," he explained. "If we can remove that, we'll shut down the whole plant."

Batman and Wonder Woman looked at J'onn hopefully, as if his simple statement came with a plan attached to it.

"I'll need a diversion," the Martian Manhunter said.

"You've got it," Batman replied, pulling out a Batarang and tossing it in one smooth motion.

The spinning disc sped though the air, slicing open a thick pipe. The ruptured vein oozed black oily gunk onto the aliens below. As panic spread among the stunned workers, Wonder Woman tore another pipe from its place in the wall, causing sparks and smoke to erupt and spread through the cavern.

Taking advantage of these diversions, J'onn J'onzz shifted into a semitransparent state, dropping down through the floor as a plasma blast passed right through the spot where he had been standing. Rising back through the floor in front of the Ion Matrix Crystal, J'onn resolidified his body, surprising the alien guarding the crystal. A quick, well-placed blow to the neck disposed of the guard, and the Martian Manhunter grabbed the crystal from the console on which it rested.

WHIRR-WHIRR-WHIRR-WHIRR-whirr . . .

The cacophonous noise wound down as the massive complex ground to a halt, its throbbing pumps now silent. Aliens scrambled in fear and confusion as J'onn raced back toward his team-mates, the enormous crystal cradled delicately in his arms.

Scrambling to his feet, the guard blasted J'onn in the back, sending the Martian Manhunter sprawling to the ground. The Ion Matrix Crystal rolled from his grip.

"J'onn!" Wonder Woman shouted from across the complex. Without removing her gaze from her fallen comrade, Diana lashed out with both fists simultaneously, leveling two guards charging from either side. Flying swiftly to J'onn's aid, she lifted him into her arms.

"Get him out!" Batman shouted, flipping a guard

over his shoulder and bowling over two technicians. "Now!"

Two soldiers stepped into Wonder Woman's path. Taking to the air, she flew right into them, crashing through the aliens, soaring for the exit that now began to close quickly, in identical fashion to the other swirling membrances, attempting to seal its prisoners inside.

Spotting the rapidly closing exit, Batman dashed for the door, then stopped as something caught his attention. Stooping over the fallen crystal, Batman scooped it into his hands, then resumed his race for the door.

Slipping though the membrane just as it closed, Wonder Woman carried J'onn to safety. Turning back, she saw the sealed exit—with Batman trapped on the other side. "Batman?" she asked, hardly believing that the incredibly resourceful Dark Knight had not found some way to make it out in time.

Clutching the crystal with one hand, Batman pounded on the sealed membrane with his other fist, unable to move the now solid closure. Spinning around in frustration, he found himself surrounded by alien guards, who trained their plasma rifles on him. Batman tossed the crystal to his captors, and it rolled along the ground to their feet. Then he braced himself for the coming battle.

On the other side of the door, with J'onn recovering nearby, Wonder Woman watched in horror as the wall she had just passed through buckled from the many impacts of plasma blasts fired from the other side.

"No!" she screamed, rushing back to the door.

J'onn reached out and grabbed her arm. "Wait!" he cried. "There is nothing more we can do for him."

Staring at the door, Diana saw no more movement, heard no sound—no blasts, no struggle, no last-second heroics.

Looking up at J'onn, her mind filled with rage and dread, she whispered, "You don't mean he's—he's...?"

"Gone." J'onn completed her thought, nodding grimly.

Fighting back tears, she leaned against the misshapen wall. In the short time she had known Batman, Diana had come to respect his experience, knowledge, and intelligence. He was a true warrior of the highest order, and she felt that somehow he would find a way to survive.

Surprised by the depth of feeling she had so quickly developed for these mortals, Princess Diana looked up. "Hera, help us," she whispered softly.

CHAPTER 8

At the WayneTech radar substation on the outskirts of Metropolis, repairs to the damaged satellite dish had been going on for many months and were now nearing completion. It was essential for the military to re-establish its deep-space monitoring capabilities. The world could not afford to get caught off guard again by the arrival of any additional invading aliens.

Deep rumbles of thunder rolled across the complex and shafts of lightning split the black sky. A lone technician balanced on the huge dish, welding the final connections into place, pausing every so often to glance up at the ominous, unnatural darkness.

Lifting his welding visor, wiping the sweat from his forehead with the sleeve of his lab coat, the technician signaled a colleague who was waiting inside the installation's control room.

"Done," he reported into a two-way radio under his visor. "The last connection. I thought we'd never get this dish back online. You should be getting readings by now."

"Are you sure you hooked it up right?" came the static-filled reply through his headset.

Double-checking his last few welds, the technician responded. "Yeah, it's all correct," he said. "Why?"

"My readings are off the chart," the technician monitoring the control panel explained. "Something's coming this way from deep space. Something big. I mean really big!"

A few miles away in downtown Metropolis, Snapper Carr continued his round-the-clock coverage of the invasion. Standing in front of the ion factory, Carr spoke into his handheld microphone, at the same time receiving constant updates from his producers back at the WGBS newsroom through a small earpiece.

"I've just received a report that government sources have confirmed the approach of another object from space," he announced. The smokestacks pouring black energy into the sky were visible behind him. "Based on readings from our deep-space monitoring system, they believe this object is roughly five times the size of the first asteroids to crash into the Earth." Carr turned and gestured to the ion factory, then looked back at the camera.

"Senator J. Allen Carter has urged the public to remain calm in light of this new development," he reported.

Several blocks away, the public was anything but calm. The anxiety and tension that had filled the city since the time of the alien landing had finally boiled over into violence. Looters rampaged through the shopping district, smashing windows and generally stealing or destroying anything they could get their hands on.

Crowds of people ran screaming through the streets, overturning cars, as police sirens blared in the distance. The Metropolis police force, already overburdened by days of battling the invaders, did what they could to control the crowds, but their resources were spread dangerously thin, and chaos reigned on the streets.

Pitching a rock through a store window, a young man reached through the shattered storefront and grabbed a small television set, tucking it under his arm. "I always wanted one of these," he said to his buddy, who looked around nervously, expecting the police to arrive at any second.

"But what if we get caught?" he asked anxiously.

"What difference does it make?" the man with the TV shot back as the two disappeared around a corner. "The world's coming to an end anyway!"

From a nearby rooftop, J'onn J'onzz and Wonder Woman looked down on the violence, destruction, and utter lawlessness.

"Perhaps Mother was right about mankind," Wonder Woman said sadly. Below, a raving man tossed a metal garbage can through a window, then simply continued down the street. "They are nothing but untamed savages."

J'onn J'onzz watched with calm detachment and a hint of compassion in his large eyes. "Do not judge them too harshly, Princess," he advised. "They act out of fear, and fear usually brings out the worst in all of us."

Nearby, two men struggled in vain to lift an

enormous chunk of concrete that had fallen from a shattered building. As they strained to move the slab, a crowd of rioters ran past, screaming and throwing bottles.

"Hey!" shouted one of the men, looking away from his task for a moment. "There are two kids trapped under here. Someone give us a hand!"

Ignoring the desperate plea, the shrieking mob raced past, caught up in the bedlam and destruction that had overtaken the streets.

Turning back to their hopeless undertaking, the man and his friend braced their shoulders against the base of the slab and heaved, their faces red, veins bulging from their straining necks, to no avail. The concrete tomb refused to budge.

Suddenly an emerald light from above surrounded the concrete piece, lifting it into the air like a giant, powerful hand, revealing two terrified six-year-olds huddled in a doorway, their faces masks of fright and disbelief.

The man who had cried for help looked up as the Green Lantern placed the concrete wall harmlessly on the street and silently flew away.

"Thanks, man!" the relieved rescuer shouted.

Helping the traumatized children to their feet, the two men quickly led them to safety.

Wonder Woman and J'onn J'onzz waited, concerned about the lateness of their teammates. Gliding gently to the rooftop, Green Lantern landed beside the heroes. A few seconds later, the Flash streaked straight up the side of the tall building to join the group.

"Sorry we're late," Green Lantern said. "Had to stop and help some civilians."

"So, what did you call us back for, anyway, J'onn?" Flash asked, referring to the telepathic message that had brought the duo racing back from the Malaysian jungle before their task had been completed.

"Superman's been captured," Wonder Woman explained. "He's trapped somewhere inside there with Hawkgirl." She pointed to the mammoth ion factory towering above the rooftops a short distance away, its exterior pumping chambers beating in rhythm, black clouds still billowing from the lofty smokestacks.

"Whoa!" Flash exclaimed, staring at the complex. "That one looks even nastier than the one we just left."

"And what about Batman?" Green Lantern asked, fearing the worst.

Sighing deeply, Wonder Woman lowered her head. Her entire body seemed to deflate. She couldn't bring herself to convey the news.

J'onn J'onzz looked right at Green Lantern, shaking his head. "He acted heroically to the very end," he said sadly. "His sacrifice enabled us to escape."

Stunned, Flash stepped back as if he had been punched in the midsection. "The Bat's gone? Really gone?" As Wally West, he had worshiped Batman ever since he was a kid, tagging along with the previous Flash, Barry Allen. Barry's death had shaken young Wally to his core, but somehow he had been able to pull himself together and get on with his life. Although he'd lost his mentor, heroes such as the Batman inspired Wally and helped him stay focused on his life's purpose as a super hero.

Once he took on the responsibilities of being the Fastest Man Alive, Wally joked about the Dark Knight's serious attitude and grim demeanor. But underneath he had nothing but respect for the protector of Gotham. He hoped to one day be as great a hero, but now he'd have to do it without the great detective.

"He was a true warrior," Wonder Woman said softly, finally able to speak.

Green Lantern's face tightened, grim determination masking his pain. He had seen more than his share of death, even the loss of close friends, but it never got any easier. Burying his feelings of dread beneath the armor of his chiseled exterior, he turned to the others.

"This is not good," he growled. "Definitely not good."

After absorbing the devastating news as best as they could and regaining their composure, the four heroes made their way to the ion factory. Crouching silently behind the wall of a damaged building, they peered at the menacing structure, which was far more threatening up close.

"I can't believe we're doing this again!" Flash whispered nervously.

"If Superman and Hawkgirl are in there, someone's gotta rescue them," Green Lantern pointed out, no more pleased about another attempt to break into a factory than his less experienced colleague. He turned to J'onn. "You *are* sure they're still in there, aren't you?" he asked.

Once again, J'onn slipped into a telepathic trance,

his eyes glowing orange, his face and body motionless, no sign of breathing.

"J'onn?" Green Lantern asked again. "Did you hear me?"

J'onn's eyes stopped glowing and his chest heaved slightly as his breathing returned to normal. "Yes," he replied, having heard every word. "Your friends are still alive, but we must act quickly. The Imperium is coming."

"The who?" Flashed asked, wondering if he would ever understand anything this weird Martian guy said.

"The Imperium," J'onn repeated. "A supreme central intelligence that controls these invaders. He is also in psychic command of this organically created factory, as if it were one of his soldiers." Looking into the blackened sky, he added solemnly, "We have met before."

Flash grabbed Green Lantern's elbow and pulled him a few steps to the side. "Think we can trust this space case?" he asked in a low voice.

"What choice do we have?" the Emerald Warrior whispered back. He quickly turned to the others. "Okay, we're going in. Flash, create a diversion. Diana, watch my back."

Arching an eyebrow, Wonder Woman shot a puzzled look at Green Lantern. "You want to rely on an 'amateur'?"

Ignoring her barb, Green Lantern shouted, "Let's move!"

Bursting from his hiding place, Flash tore across the charred pavement, streaking past a walker pod. Stopping suddenly, the Scarlet Speedster grabbed a rock and pitched it at the walker, striking the pod high above ground level.

"Tag, you're it!" he shouted, sticking out his tongue and blowing a raspberry at the monstrous machine, which turned and fired a round of plasma blasts at him.

Moving at blinding speed, Flash avoided each searing beam and led the walker away from the factory, keeping its attention focused on him. "Missed me!" he taunted. "Not even close!"

Zigzagging back and forth in front of the walker, then circling around it a few times for good measure, Flash led his adversary toward a large mound near the edge of the clearing created by the emergence of the factory.

"Come on, slowpoke!" he shouted, standing next to the mound, waving his crimson-clad arms. "I dare you to catch me. Over here!"

Close to its target now, the walker lifted its huge leg, bringing it down swiftly, trying to crush Flash where he stood. Zooming out of the way at the last second, Flash stopped, turned, and watched the walker step on the mound, a land-mine nodule identical to the one Flash himself had tripped at the factory in the jungle.

THOOM!

The mine erupted in a geyser of goo, the explosive force blowing off the bottom third of the walker's leg.

"Oops!" Flash cried, pretending to stifle an exaggerated giggle. "You really stepped in it this time!"

Wobbling as it struggled to regain balance, the walker toppled to the ground, shattering upon impact.

"Buh-bye," Flash said, grinning and waving his fingers, then zipping away in a blur.

Green Lantern, Wonder Woman, and J'onn J'onzz took full advantage of the distraction Flash provided, flying into the hole in the factory wall that Superman had created earlier.

"J'onn, where are Superman and Hawkgirl being held?" Green Lantern asked once they were inside, navigating the maze of organic, veinlike corridors.

The Martian Manhunter's eyes glowed for a moment, then returned to normal. "This way," he said, pointing down a narrow passageway.

As the three heroes landed, proceeding on foot, Flash zoomed up beside them. "Hope I didn't keep you," he said, grinning and falling into step with the others.

Voices up ahead stopped the group in its tracks. J'onn motioned for his companions to get out of sight. "Wait here," he said as the others pressed their backs against a damp, fleshy wall.

As his teammates watched in amazement, J'onn abandoned his human form, morphing into an exact likeness of an invader, tall and fluid, patches of gray and red amorphously shifting on his milky white exterior. Racing down a corridor, J'onn approached two alien guards.

"Cha porna tee orta!" he shouted, informing them of a break-in, pointing in the direction of his friends. As the guards rushed past him, J'onn reverted to his familiar human-like form. Turning semitransparent, he dropped into the ground beneath his feet. Moving slowly through the solid rock, the Martian Manhunter headed toward his friends.

Farther up the passage, the aliens came upon Wonder Woman, Green Lantern, and Flash, all pressed tightly against the wall. The guards raised their weapons, aiming them at the heroes.

J'onn, still in his semitransparent form, rose through the ground, silently emerging behind the aliens. He shoved his fists through their backs, then resolidified his body.

"Aiiiiii!" the invaders shrieked in pain as J'onn's now-solid arms struck them like jackhammers. Turning semitransparent again, J'onn removed his arms from the guards' bodies. They crumpled to the ground, unconscious.

Assuming his solid form again, J'onn motioned for the others to follow. "Come," he said, racing back around the corner.

Flash glanced at his two teammates, each of whom met his frightened, amazed, and skeptical gaze with astonished looks of their own. "Is it just me?" he asked. "Or does he creep you out, too?"

Leading the others through the labyrinth of corridors, J'onn came to a sudden stop at what appeared to be a sealed doorway blending into the walls on either side. He placed his palms flat against the wall, and his eyes glowed for a moment.

"We are close now," he reported. "I sense they are just beyond these walls."

Pressing her shoulder against the door, Wonder Woman strained with all her considerable might, but the entryway refused to budge. Stepping back, exhaling in exhaustion and frustration, she shook her head. "It's no use," she admitted. "We'll have to find another way through."

"Stand clear," Green Lantern said, raising his power ring. Using a fine beam from the ring like a welding torch, he sliced a small hole in the doorway. Moving the beam slowly outward, he proceeded to cut a large circle in the door.

As Green Lantern worked, J'onn turned quickly, as if listening for sounds in the distance, his eyes glowing again briefly. "We haven't much time left," he announced.

Outside the factory, a deafening roar, like endless thunder, echoed through the concrete canyons, shattering windows and splitting steel as deadly debris tumbled to the sidewalks.

Looters and rioters stopped their destruction and stared up in terror at the latest arrival in this seemingly eternal invasion. A young man who had just pulled a radio from a shattered shop window pointed to the sky.

Thick black clouds parted, making way for an enormous spaceship three football fields long that slowly descended toward the ion factory. Its immense shadow, cast by the nonstop flashing of lightning, covered the shrouded city in an even deeper layer of darkness.

Back in the factory, Green Lantern's power beam completed its journey around the doorway. Aiming for the center of the circle he had sliced, Green Lantern kicked the door, and the round cut-out piece fell inward, dropping to the floor in the chamber beyond.

"We're in!" he shouted, stepping through the hole, followed closely by the others.

The shocking sight that greeted the heroes froze them in their tracks. Dangling upside down from the ceiling, Superman and Hawkgirl hung helplessly, their feet embedded in the tissue-like roof of the chamber, their eyes closed.

"Great Hera!" Wonder Woman exclaimed, rushing toward her trapped teammates with Green Lantern and Flash by her side.

J'onn J'onzz waited, cautiously surveying the cavernous chamber. "Wait!" he shouted as the others raced forward. "Something is not right."

As if in reaction to J'onn's warning, Superman suddenly opened his eyes. An orange glow flashed from the gleaming orbs.

"Whoa!" Flash cried, slamming on the brakes, stopping just short of the dangling figures.

Behind them, the hole that Green Lantern had cut sealed itself, oozing closed like a wound healing at incredible speed. Small pores opened in the walls all around them, flooding the chamber with choking venomous gas. "It's a trap!" Green Lantern shouted, falling to his knees.

"Lantern, your ring," Wonder Woman gasped, losing her balance, tumbling to the ground.

"Can't focus," Green Lantern wheezed. "The gas. I, I—"

Within seconds the four heroes lay sprawled on the chamber floor, unconscious. "Superman" and "Hawkgirl" dropped from the ceiling, flipping onto their feet, cackling maliciously at the fallen champions.

Morphing back into their true forms, the aliens resumed their red, gray, and black appearance. *"Da far-toe gool,"* one alien screeched, then helped the other carry the four limp bodies from the chamber.

CHAPTER

9

J'onn J'onzz regained consciousness slowly. The sound of relentless pounding from the factory's heartlike energy pumps filled his head, penetrating the haze of confusion caused by the gas. Trying to move his arms and legs, J'onn discovered they were tightly bound in a thick, weblike membrane coating the factory's walls.

Forcing his eyes open, J'onn saw that he was back in the central core. The Ion Matrix Crystal, which the invaders had taken back from Batman, was now in place to power the complex, which extended around the world. The factory buzzed with the activity of hundreds of aliens busily going about their work.

Glancing to his left and right, J'onn saw his five

teammates all bound in similar fashion, their arms and legs embedded in the glistening membrane. Then he quickly lost consciousness again.

Superman awakened next.

Having been born under the red sun of the planet Krypton, Superman drew his great powers from Earth's yellow sun. As the aliens covered the sky with thick black clouds, less and less of the sun's energy reached the Man of Steel. With each passing hour, he felt more of his superstrength drain from his body.

In his weakened state, Superman had become vulnerable to the effects of the alien gas. He had been trapped in the membrane for many hours, with Hawkgirl imprisoned beside him, drifting in and out of consciousness, unable to use his superstrength to break free.

Forcing his eyes open, sizing up the situation, the Man of Steel realized quickly that things had gotten worse. Now six heroes were trapped, and Batman was nowhere to be seen. He tried to focus his heat vision on the membrane that held him, but his power was too drained for him to use that ability either.

"J'onn," he called out, seeing the Martian Manhunter fade back into unconsciousness. "J'onn, wake up!"

J'onn's eyes snapped open again.

"You shouldn't have risked your lives for us," Superman said, tugging mightily in another vain attempt to free his arms.

"Would you have done less for me?" J'onn replied as the others began to awaken.

"Oh, my aching head," Flash moaned. "Remind me never to order that again, whatever it was I had."

One by one, the heroes regained consciousness. As the captives looked on in shock, Senator J. Allen Carter stepped from the shadows.

"Senator Carter?" Superman asked, confused. "What are you doing here?"

Carter smiled his famous charismatic smile. "Unfortunately, Superman, the real Carter never returned from Mars two years ago," he explained. "Although he was kind enough to release us from our prison there."

As the heroes watched in astonishment, Carter revealed his true identity, morphing into an alien invader.

Superman felt the fury building inside him as he realized the true meaning of the events of the past six months. "You used me to weaken Earth's defenses!" he shouted angrily.

"And you were so eager to cooperate," the alien said, grinning triumphantly as he morphed back into the form of Senator Carter. "Thanks to you, the humans were totally helpless against us."

Enraged, Superman struggled fiercely to break free, but his diminished strength fell just short. "It's not over yet," the Man of Steel snarled.

"Wrong again, Superman," Carter said confidently, pointing up.

A small section of the factory's roof slowly slid open to reveal the enormous spaceship hovering above, blocking out the sky. Landing-bay doors on the ship's bottom slid open, and a small shuttle drifted out and lowered steadily. Passing through the open roof, the shuttle came to rest on a rock outcropping near the Ion Matrix Crystal overlooking the trapped heroes.

Carter urgently ran to the ship, all thoughts of his captives suddenly overshadowed by his sense of duty and loyalty to the powerful creature within.

"All hail the Imperium!" Carter shouted, bowing deeply.

"Hoch na perum!" a chorus of alien voices repeated in their own tongue, each invader bowing as well.

A large, transparent, bloblike being emerged from a hatchway in the bottom of the shuttle craft and drifted through the air toward Carter. A collection of swirling gases and liquids sparkled and shifted within the creature's glowing purple membrane, rippling from the movement within. Long pink and black tentacles extending from the body reached out as it moved forward.

Floating right past the alien who appeared to be Senator Carter, the Imperium briefly acknowledged its faithful servant, then slithered toward the trapped heroes.

Superman stared at the creature, which looked nothing like the horde of aliens who worshiped it, and realized he had seen this thing before. Glancing at J'onn, whose eyes were fixed upon the Imperium, the Man of Steel finally remembered where he had seen this being—it was in one of the psychic messages from J'onn. It was one of the many images that had flooded his mind. Now, what had seemed more like a nightmare than a reality hovered before him menacingly.

The Imperium's voice filled J'onn's mind. *"J'onn J'onzz,"* the deep rumbling voice said, echoing inside the Martian's skull. *"It's been a long time."*

Struggling unsuccessfully to keep the Imperium out of his head, J'onn turned away in disgust.

At a telepathic signal from the Imperium, the membrane that held J'onn separated from the wall. It reached up like a long arm and deposited him on the ledge, right in front of the creature, who motioned to two alien guards nearby.

The guards approached J'onn, each carrying a prodlike weapon. Jabbing the helpless hero in his ribs, they unleashed savage electric jolts, which surged through J'onn's body, searing his insides.

"Aaaagh!" he screamed, writhing in pain. Losing his ability to maintain his Earth-friendly shape, J'onn reverted to his natural Martian form, his long spindly limbs flailing and his pointed cranium twitching wildly.

At a second subtle command from the Imperium, the guards removed their prods. J'onn immediately collapsed to the ground, electricity still coursing through his wracked body.

"Much better," the Imperium spoke again directly into J'onn's mind, now clouded with pain and confusion. *"You have defied us for centuries."*

Struggling to regain control of his own thoughts, J'onn replied telepathically. *"And I will never bow before you or any of your kind."*

"Then I will personally see to finishing what should have been finished long ago," the Imperium replied, slithering closer to the Martian.

The monstrous creature extended sharp tendrils, smaller and more muscular than its main tentacles. Piercing J'onn's skin, the pointed limbs entered his arms and chest, worming their way up through his body toward his brain.

"Arrrggghh!" J'onn shrieked, feeling as if his head would explode from the pain.

"Our mission, started these many centuries ago, will finally be complete," the Imperium said, forcing his booming voice into J'onn's burning skull, *"when I have eliminated the last Martian."*

Pulling J'onn toward him, his jagged tendrils still embedded deep within the Martian's body, the Imperium drew J'onn through his amorphous outer membrane, sucking him into his bloblike central section. The prisoner's shrill cries of pain were muffled by the creature's viscous interior body fluids.

Superman thrashed violently against the restraining membrane, enraged and frustrated by his inability to help his tortured friend. "Let go of him!" he cried helplessly.

Tightening his grip on J'onn's agonized brain, the Imperium shouted into his captive's mind. *"Yield to me, J'onn J'onzz!"* he commanded.

"Never!" J'onn screamed back defiantly.

"Why do you resist?" the Imperium asked, a tone of mock concern in his telepathic voice. *"Embrace this truth. After all these years, you have finally lost."*

Mustering every scrap of his strength, J'onn remained defiant. *"Have I?"* he asked, an unexpected edge of confidence coloring his question. *"Are you certain?"*

The Imperium shuddered, sensing something disturbing deep within J'onn's mind. *"You're hiding something,"* he bellowed. *"A secret deep in the recesses of your mind."*

Sensing the panic washing over his adversary, J'onn buried his secret even deeper.

"Is this another one of your cursed Martian tricks?" the Imperium raged.

"Do I sense fear from the great Imperium?" J'onn asked mockingly.

"I can stand this deception no longer," the Imperium blustered, anger and fear coursing through the synaptic circuits of his gel-like mass. *"What are you hiding?"*

Telepathically tapping into the nerve impulses firing past him as he floated within the Imperium, J'onn sensed his enemy's weakness and knew that the time was right for action. Morphing back into his more human form, he shouted, "Now!"

An explosion near the Ion Matrix Crystal rocked the central core chamber and tore a gaping hole in the console that held the power source in place. Rising from the smoke, Batman suddenly appeared, climbing through the hole created by his explosive. He crouched on the console, a small rectangular device clutched firmly in his left hand.

"Batman?" Flash asked in wonder.

"It can't be!" Wonder Woman cried.

Batman reached out and attached the device he had created directly onto the Ion Matrix Crystal. As energy surged from the small mechanism into the glowing crystal, the crystal's color gradually faded from black to brilliant white. The trapped heroes looked on in wonder while panic spread through the aliens, who felt the sudden change deep within their beings.

Flipping a switch on the device he had placed onto the crystal, Batman fired a grappling line, which embedded itself in a crevice above. Rising swiftly on the line, away from the crystal's console, Batman watched as a glowing blue energy shield appeared, surrounding the crystal and its ion-reversal device.

Guards opened fire at the Caped Crusader, who deftly dodged the blasts.

"What have you done!" Carter shouted up at Batman from the edge of the outcropping.

"What trickery is this?" the Imperium demanded.

"I mentally shielded Batman so he couldn't be detected by you or any of your invaders," J'onn explained. *"He was working undercover to find your weakness, and it appears that he has done just that!"*

J'onn then sent a telepathic message to his friends. *"I apologize for the deception, but it was important that all of you believed Batman was dead. That way the invaders couldn't learn the truth if they searched your minds."*

"The crystal!" the Imperium bellowed to his soldiers in a furious rage. "Destroy it!"

Unleashing a barrage of plasma blasts, the invaders fired at the crystal, attempting to carry out the Imperium's order. The searing laser discharges bounced harmlessly off the gleaming blue energy shield.

"They've shielded the crystal!" shrieked Carter, watching in horror as streaming white energy crackled, forcing intense bright light up through the factory's ducts.

Outside, the towering smokestacks suddenly stopped belching black fumes, instead discharging radiant, shimmering white energy, which cut through the murky clouds, dissipating their blanket of darkness. Golden sunlight streamed through the breaks in the clouds, bathing the streets of Metropolis with warmth and illumination, and raising the spirit of the desperate populace for the first time in days.

Piercing shafts of sunlight also poured into the factory through the large opening in its roof. As the honey-colored beams struck the invaders, their bodies instantly burst into flames, melted into puddles of goo, then finally evaporated in a waft of steam.

J'onn J'onzz felt the Imperium weakening. He mustered all his strength and burst free from the creature's body, taking advantage of the terror coursing through its nervous system. As alien soldiers scrambled for cover from the searing sunlight, J'onn grabbed the Imperium's tentacles, dragging him from the shadows.

"No!" the Imperium cried as its outer membrane blistered upon contact with the light.

"You live underground and shun all light," J'onn, now clearly in control, shouted at the being, which moments before had been his living prison. "Why? Does it burn?"

Smoke and flames rose from the Imperium's membrane, its liquid interior reaching the boiling point, a bubbling mass of burning organic tissue. *"Chaaaaaa!"* the alien shrieked as the Martian Manhunter held it beneath the rays of sunlight.

Wincing in revulsion from the gruesome sight, Flash turned away. "Ooh, man, that's one nasty sunburn," he cracked, his feet still embedded in the wall.

The Imperium struggled for his life, desperately trying to free himself from the grasp of J'onn J'onzz. With their leader unable to focus on anything but his own survival, the alien soldiers raced frantically through the factory, seeking refuge from the sunlight, thinking only of their own lives.

Batman took advantage of the chaos. Swooping down on his grappling line, he pulled a small but powerful pocket laser from his Utility Belt.

"It is good to see you alive," Wonder Woman said as the Dark Knight sliced through the fleshlike membrane on the wall with his laser's tightly focused beam, freeing her arms and legs.

As sunlight poured into the factory, Superman felt his strength returning. He didn't often think about the source of his powers. In some ways he took it for granted. He was, after all, Superman. He could simply do these amazing things. But now, having been weakened by the blocking of the sun, the Man of Steel felt a great sense of relief as power once again flowed through his body.

Flexing his reenergized muscles, he tore his arms and legs free of the binding membrane, then set about helping Batman release the others.

"That was a pretty neat trick," the Man of Steel said to his longtime friend as he used his heat vision to cut open the membrane that held the Flash. "What did you do to the crystal?"

"I reversed the ion charge," the Dark Knight replied

casually. "That in turn reversed the effect of the energy the invaders had been pouring into the skies."

"Slick move, Bats," Flash said as he rubbed his newly freed wrists. "We thought we'd lost you there for a second. Welcome back."

Batman turned a puzzled glance to Flash as he cut Green Lantern's hand free with his tiny laser. He was not used to being referred to so casually, yet he sensed genuine relief in the Flash's tone. Shrugging it off, he sliced open the membrane that held the Emerald Warrior's feet.

"Likewise," Green Lantern said, clasping Batman's shoulder warmly. "It's just not the same without you."

Superman used his heat vision to cut Hawkgirl's arms free from the membrane. Before he could turn the searing beams to the membrane near her feet, the Winged Warrior swung her mace, slashing the fleshy wall, releasing her own feet.

"How did you know that sunlight would hurt the creatures?" Hawkgirl asked Batman, stretching her cramped limbs.

"I began to suspect something when I first entered the factory in Egypt," the Dark Knight explained. "I noticed the aliens running from sunlight. Using a skin sample I took from an alien I defeated in that factory, I returned to the Batcave, where my research led me to the conclusion that the ultraviolet rays in sunlight are deadly to their species. Coming from the depths of space, the invaders have no resistance to our sun's radiation."

"That's why they needed these factories," Superman said, keeping a watchful eye out for alien guards. "They had to block out the sun."

"Yes," Batman agreed. "I created the ion-reversal device and used their own factories against them."

"So you did find their weakness after all," Wonder Woman added. "Impressive."

Across the cavernous chamber, the Imperium was still firmly in the grasp of J'onn J'onzz, and still burning up from the sun's rays. But the sight of the super heroes, now free, enraged him, giving him a momentary burst of strength. "Destroy them, you cowards!" he shouted to his fleeing troops in a voice choked and strained. "Even at the cost of your own lives!"

As the alien soldiers opened fire, Superman flew swiftly to the foot of a ledge a short distance away. Grabbing the rocklike formation, he bent the pliable tissue up toward the attacking invaders, forming a protective wall between the soldiers and his friends.

As the alien's plasma blasts bounced harmlessly off the wall, the heroes began an improvised counter-offensive, buoyed by the sudden reversal of fortune, glad to be finally released from their bonds.

Hawkgirl took to the air, flying straight for a group of soldiers who stood firing randomly on a nearby bluff. Swinging her energy-charged mace in whirl-wind circles, the Winged Warrior slammed into the aliens, obliterating them in seconds.

As if celebrating the release of his speedy feet, Flash zoomed right through the center of a squadron of aliens. The rippling effect of the wind he created flung them across the chamber on either side.

Powering up his ring, Green Lantern surrounded a trio of aliens with a green force field just as they fired their weapons. The plasma blasts, contained by the force field, baked the invaders alive.

Superman flew straight up, leading with his fists. He tore a jagged hole right through the top of the factory's dome, then emerged into the brightness beyond. Sunlight poured through the new hole in the roof, searing the screeching aliens caught in its radiant beams.

Following suit, Wonder Woman and Green Lantern each took to the air, tearing additional huge holes in the dome, flooding even more of the chamber with brilliant sunlight.

Realizing that its life force was draining rapidly in the increasing glare of the sun's rays, the Imperium—its body bubbling furiously, its outer membrane almost gone—shot its jagged tendrils into J'onn's body again, lifting the Martian off his feet.

Shrieking in pain as the tendrils once again surged through his body, J'onn lost consciousness. Withdrawing its tendrils quickly, the Imperium allowed its adversary to crumble to the ground in a heap as it floated back toward the waiting shuttle craft.

Seeing this, Carter—who had stood his ground by firing plasma blasts at the rallying heroes—leapt into the air. Grabbing hold of the Imperium's body, he dangled by his scorched fingertips as the flaming creature rose toward its shuttle. "My Imperium!" Carter shouted. "Take me with you!"

"Unhand me, worm!" the Imperium blustered, slapping Carter off with a whipping tentacle, sending the imposter sprawling to the ground.

Landing in a pool of sunlight, the alien who had posed as Carter blistered, flames spreading across his skin, which now reverted to its true appearance. For two years he had fooled the world, disguised as J. Allen Carter, tricking Superman into disarming Earth's most powerful weapons, leading the planet to the brink of destruction.

"Nooo!" the alien now screamed as his flesh melted into a molten pool of white, gray, and red, then boiled into vapor and disappeared.

Soaring through the air, dodging alien fire, Wonder Woman spotted the Imperium drifting into the open hatch at the bottom of the shuttle. Watching the doors slide shut and the craft fire its main thrusters, the Amazon Princess darted toward the ship as it rose through the opening in the factory's roof.

Unfurling her Golden Lasso, Wonder Woman hurled the glittering rope toward the departing space-craft. Looping around an angled protrusion on the bottom of the shuttle, the lasso found its target. Tightening the loop, Wonder Woman pulled on the magic rope, straining to stop the rising ship.

A plasma blast from the shuttle's laser cannon knocked Wonder Woman off her feet. The small craft cleared the factory, then rose toward the giant warship above, Diana's Golden Lasso dangling from its bottom.

Hawkgirl flew after the escaping craft, bashing a hole in its front panel with her mace. Smoke poured from the hole, and the ship shuddered but continued drifting toward the warship, which now opened its landing-bay doors in anticipation of the Imperium's arrival.

Shaking off the blow dealt by the laser cannon, an angry Wonder Woman flew back up to the shuttle, grabbing her lasso and tugging the craft back down just as it was about to enter the warship.

With Wonder Woman holding the shuttle in place, Hawkgirl unleashed four more powerful blows to the sputtering ship. The last wallop from her mace finally sent the smoking shuttle plunging back toward the factory below.

Crashing through the roof, the shuttle careened toward Batman, who looked up—helplessly realizing he had no time to get out of the way.

From the corner of his eye, Batman caught sight of a scarlet streak. Before his brain had fully processed this tidbit of visual information, the Dark Knight found himself in Flash's arms, being carried to safety just as the Imperium's shuttle slammed to the factory's floor right in the spot where Batman had been standing. The resulting explosion cut the number of remaining aliens in half, destroying the Imperium in the process.

"I'd hate to lose you again," Flash said as he placed Batman back onto his feet.

THOOM!

A huge section of the central core collapsed in flames.

"Uh, maybe we better get out of here," Flash suggested.

Nearby, Superman, who had been helping J'onn J'onzz recover from the Imperium's final attack, pointed to a line of larval sacs hanging from the wall. "Not without them!" Superman insisted, indicating the podlike pouches.

Using his heat vision, the Man of Steel sliced open the long, translucent sacs, easing the unconscious people within gently to the floor as two alien guards across the chamber opened fire.

Almost fully recovered, J'onn J'onzz became semitransparent again and dropped through the floor. He re-emerged behind the two attackers, solidified his body, and delivered crushing blows to the aliens' heads, knocking them to the ground.

Gathering up the comatose human victims, Superman called out for help. "Flash!" he shouted. "Give me a hand!"

Rushing to Superman's side, Flash grabbed a victim by the arms, then backed away in revulsion. "Eww, gross!" he exclaimed, wiping the gelatinous organic fluid from his hands on the pants of his costume.

"Now!" Superman ordered, looking at the young hero sharply. For all his amazing ability, energy, and youthful exuberance, the junior member of the team still had a lot to learn about appropriate behavior during a crisis.

Flash then moved with remarkable speed, helping Superman collect the limp bodies into a group just as another section of the central core exploded and showered the heroes with debris.

"This whole place is going to blow!" Hawkgirl shouted, swooping down beside Superman, followed closely by Green Lantern.

"Everybody, stay close!" the Emerald Warrior shouted, powering up his ring. A huge green force field encased the unconscious bodies, then Green Lantern rose through the huge hole in the roof, carrying the victims within his protective shield.

Superman grabbed Flash and took to the air, followed closely by Wonder Woman, who was carrying Batman. Hawkgirl and J'onn J'onzz flew from the flaming factory just as a fiery explosion ripped through the central core and filled the massive chamber with smoke and flames.

Flying just ahead of the mushrooming blast, the heroes looked down to see the entire factory erupt like a volcano, then collapse in on itself in a final, violent cacophony of destruction.

Landing on the damaged roof of the Daily Planet Building beside its shattered signature globe, the victorious champions looked to the clearing sky. They saw the Imperium's massive warship—minus its leader—soar high above the city, picking up speed, then finally vanishing from view. Tracking its progress with his telescopic vision, Superman continued to observe the ship as it left the solar system and receded into the murky depths of space.

"It's over," he announced grimly, scanning the devastated city as the last dark clouds dissipated. Flickering flames and clear, brilliant sunshine illuminated the heroes. Silently they pondered their costly victory.

In the days that followed, the heroes returned to the various factory locations around the world to eliminate the remaining aliens, walker pods, and the factories themselves.

On a large monitor deep within the Batcave, Batman watched intently as taped television reports showed Superman and Wonder Woman taking out a walker in Metropolis, Green Lantern crushing the remains of the factory in Malaysia, and Hawkgirl pounding on a walker in Egypt with her mace.

Snapper Carr spoke as the final images of the war flashed across the screen.

"In the aftermath of the Metropolis meltdown, most of the invaders have retreated from Earth," Carr began. "Superman and a team of other heroes have driven out the remaining pockets of resistance and helped restore order around the world.

"Yet despite this stunning victory, there are those who warn that we must remain vigilant."

The figure of General Welles filled the screen, his face weary from days of fighting a hopeless, round-the-clock battle. "We got lucky this time— if you can call it that," the general said, his voice hoarse. "But what will we do if the invaders ever return?"

Switching off the broadcast, Batman leaned back in his chair, scowled, and rubbed his chin thoughtfully. *What indeed?* he thought as he turned to a nearby computer terminal, a grand plan taking shape in his imagination.

EPILOGUE

Nine months later...

The enormous silver structure hung suspended in the star-strewn blanket of space. Gleaming in the moonlight, the giant platform orbited Earth, miles above the constantly churning chaos and progress its inhabitants struggled with every day.

Standing on an observation deck, Superman gazed out a tall curved window that extended around the entire circumference of the space station. He peered down at the beautiful blue globe that was his adopted home.

"Incredible," he muttered to himself, basking in the breathtaking view. Hearing footsteps, the Man of Steel turned to see Batman stride onto the deck.

"Do your WayneTech stockholders know about this little home away from home, Bruce?" Superman asked his longtime friend.

"A line item hidden in the aerospace research and development budget," Batman explained. His life as billionaire industrialist Bruce Wayne often intersected with his life as Batman. His wealth and standing in the international business community had distinct advantages for his role as a crime-fighting detective. "This Watchtower will act as an early warning system for detecting other threats of invasion from space."

An elevator door whooshed open and Flash and Wonder Woman stepped out onto the observation deck, each sipping a drink through a straw. "And it also has a fully stocked kitchen," Flash pointed out, extending a glass to Superman. "Iced mocha?" he offered.

"No thanks," the Man of Steel replied.

Wonder Woman took a deep sip. "Mmm, they don't have these on Themyscira," she admitted.

As if on cue, Flash zoomed to her side. "Stick around, Princess. I'll show you the ropes," he said, pointing a thumb confidently at himself.

Diana had gotten used to Flash's humor, now slightly less overbearing than at first since the brash youngster had shared a taste of life-or-death combat with the Amazon Warrior. She smiled at him.

"Perhaps I will," she replied.

Completing their tour of the Watchtower, Green Lantern and Hawkgirl descended to the observation deck, landing beside the others.

"An impressive installation," Green Lantern reported. "Most impressive. But what's it got to do with us?"

Superman stared down at the Earth for a few moments, then replied. "I once thought I could protect the world by myself," he began in a subdued tone. "But I was wrong. We saved the planet only by working together.

"I believe that if we stay together, as a team, we would be an unbeatable force that could truly fight for the ideals of peace and justice."

"What?" Flash asked, skeptically. "Like a bunch of super friends?"

Superman smiled. "More like a Justice League," he replied.

"Do you have any idea how corny that sounds?"

Flash said, stepping up beside the Man of Steel. "But maybe the big guy's got a point. With all of us behind it, this Justice League could work." He extended his hand. "Count me in."

"Me too," Green Lantern said, stepping forward and placing his hand on top of the two already clasped in a firm handshake.

"And me," Hawkgirl announced, adding her hand to the group.

Hesitating for a moment, Wonder Woman joined the circle of heroes. "My mother may not approve," she began, imagining Queen Hippolyta's reaction, "but I find man's world intriguing. I'll gladly join."

"What about you, Batman?" Superman asked, noticing his old friend standing a distance away, running diagnostics on the space station's monitoring equipment.

"I prefer to work alone," the Dark Knight replied, turning to look at the group. "I'm really not a people person, as Superman can tell you. But when you need help—and you will—call me."

"Understood," Superman said. He looked each member of the newly formed team in the eyes. "Then we're all agreed?"

"Wait," Wonder Woman said, glancing around the observation deck. "J'onn's not here."

"Yeah," Flash added. "Where is that guy?"

Standing alone on an upper level of the Watchtower, J'onn J'onzz stared out a small window, deep in thought. He was pleased that the invaders had finally been defeated, but the victory was bittersweet nonetheless. Guarding against their reawakening had consumed his life for five centuries, and he now pondered his purpose in the universe. Returning to his lifeless home world was pointless, yet he wondered if he could actually live among humans, so puzzled was he by this irrational, often violent race.

Superman drifted up to the high deck and landed silently beside the pensive Martian. "J'onn, are you all right?" he asked.

"My family and loved ones are long gone," he began wistfully. "I am the last of my kind."

"I know the feeling," Superman replied reassuringly. If anyone could relate to the Martian's situation, it was the Last Son of Krypton, who decades earlier had to come to grips with the fact that he was the sole survivor of his race.

"Mars is dead to me now, and I am alone in the universe," J'onn said sadly, lowering his head.

Superman stepped up to J'onn and gently squeezed his shoulder. "J'onn, we can never replace the family you've lost," he said, momentarily envious of the fact that at least J'onn had known his family, a privilege he had been denied. "But we'd be honored if you would join our Justice League, and could learn to call Earth your home. I know *I* have."

Looking up, J'onn smiled softly and nodded in reply. Then he and Superman returned to the group of heroes now forged into the Justice League—a team representing the best hope for the future of humankind.

ABOUT THE AUTHOR

MICHAEL TEITELBAUM has been a writer, editor, and packager of children's books, comic books, and magazines for more than twenty years. He has worked on staff as an editor at Gold Key Comics, Golden Books, Putnam/Grosset, and Macmillan. His packaging company, Town Brook Press, created and packaged *Spider-Man Magazine,* a monthly publication, for Marvel Entertainment. Michael Teitelbaum's more recent writing includes the Garfield: Pet Force books (a series of five titles), *Breaking Barriers: In Sports, In Life* (based on the life of Jackie Robinson), *Samurai Jack: The Legend Begins*, and *Batman Beyond: Return of the Joker* (all published by Scholastic); junior novels based on the feature films *Men in Black II* and *Spider-Man* (HarperCollins); and *Smallville: Arrival* (Little, Brown). Michael and his wife, Sheleigah, split their time between New York City and their 160-year-old farmhouse in upstate New York.